Presented to:

_____

By:

_____

Date: _1-14-2017_

"Where you stumble, there lies your treasure. The very cave you are afraid to enter turns out to be the source of what you are looking for. – Joseph Campbell

The Journeyman Papers

Uncommonly Grimm Lessons

Dr. John S. Nagy

The Journeyman Papers
– Uncommonly Grimm Lessons
Copyright © 2016 Dr. John S. Nagy

Also Author of:
- ✓ **The Craft Unmasked – The Uncommon Origin of Freemasonry and its Practice**
- ✓ **Building Hiram**   – Volume 1
- ✓ **Building Boaz**   – Volume 2
- ✓ **Building Athens**   – Volume 3
- ✓ **Building Janus**   – Volume 4
- ✓ **Building Perpends**   – Volume 5
- ✓ **Building Ruffish**   – Volume 6
- ✓ **Building Cement**   – Volume 7
- ✓ **Building Free Men**   – Volume 8
- ✓ **Provoking Success**
- ✓ Emotional Awareness **Made Easy**

Publisher: Promethean Genesis Publishing
PO Box 636, Lutz FL 33548-0636

ISBN-13: 978-0-9911094-3-2

First Printing, November 2016
Published in the United States of America
Book Editing, Design and Illustration
by Dr. John S. Nagy
Books available through www.coach.net

Dedication

To my family, friends and Brothers: Candy, Steven, Jeffrey, Jason Jeff, Art, Dale, Ann, Muslim, RJ, Sean, and Nick. Your encouragement and support keeps me reading, writing and sharing.

Acknowledgements

A very special thanks to the authors of the collective works of:

- The Grimm Brothers
- Joseph Campbell
- Robert Bly
- M. Scott Peck
- Rabbi Harold Kushner
- Jim Henson

Introduction

I was very young when I found myself compelled to seek out stories that drew me into imaginative worlds of long ago and far away. I loved reading or listening to the Mythologies of the Greco-Roman, Oriental and Nordic cultures, the tales of King Arthur and the Knights of the Round Table, Aesop's Fables, One Thousand and One Nights, Hans Christian Anderson's stories and the Brothers Grimm Fairy Tales. They brought to me hours of delightful sojourning within my heart and mind.

Night or day, whenever I had time, I would pull open dog-eared or bookmarked books to resume my adventures. These were years filled with enjoyment and wonder. Little did I know how well they would prepare me for what was to follow.

Many years after my youth, I found myself surrounded by a world cluttered with facts and figures very foreign to my early days. I was an adult and I did adult things. My day to day dealings were driven by the demands of doings, all revolving around my jobs, friends and family. I was fully immersed in adulthood and my childhood fantasies and pleasures became mere memories. By all outward appearances, what I held most dear in my heart during my adolescence was nowhere to be found.

Just before my thirtieth year, a series of life events re-introduced me to aspects of my soul that I had thought long gone. In those moments, I found myself searching for meaning and understanding, not just about the life that I had created for myself, but the life that I felt that I was truly meant to live.

As in my youth, I found myself compelled to seek out stories and to listen to them once again. And I listened to them, not with the eager ears of an imaginative youth, but through the tired ears of a lost soul in a wilderness of his own making.

It was a wholly different experience for me. The stories were told by masterful men, skilled in storytelling and they explained the underlying meanings entwined within each tale and their significance toward my life. Each story was not just revealed to me as potential entertainment, but also as rich fodder for the nurturing of my soul. I found myself feasting upon their words with great zeal.

As I immersed myself further in the symbolism conveyed by each tale, I found relevance with them toward my own life. I saw how the archetypes of masculine development portrayed in each of them echoed my own development in life. I saw the themes of Maturing as a backdrop for the play of superficial characters. I felt the emotions expressed directly and indirectly through the characterizations to be no different than the ones I experienced in my world. I began to recognize clearly that the symbols used as props within each story alluded to things significant to my own story. Most of all, as an adult I experienced them differently and in entirely enriching ways.

During this time of exploration and discovery, there were a few stories that stood out for me as particularly interesting. *The Devil's Sooty Brother* was one and *Bearskin* for its similarities to it. *The Gnome* was another. A few more come to mind, but for the most part, each of them reflected a specific life lesson or condition in most lives that was going to occur if lived long enough and each offered an opportunity to learn something important about ourselves, our path and our choices.

As time went on, I found that I was sharing these tales with others to read when I heard specific things going on within their lives. I would ask them to read the tale and ask themselves how these tales echo what needed to be addressed within their own lives. With relatively little discussion, it was clear from the responses I received that sharing the tales did serve a good purpose. Those who got to know them also got to know themselves better. In return, they realized they needed to make better choices and decisions and they did.

One very close friend requested I write out the tales and explain the symbols and relevance of the stories to our lives. I resisted this request in that I realized how much work was required to do so and actually felt I could not present it in a format that would do justice to it. I felt that the stories needed to be told and then retold once the symbolism was explained. This way the stories would be heard at the superficial level and then again at a much deeper level. To do this in book form would require the reader to read the story first, read through what the author would share about the underlying themes and then reread the tale from beginning to the end while making every effort to recognize how those originally unknown themes played out within an already familiar tale.

I do know that this has been done before since it was this very manner that helped me obtain a better grasp on the stories I so enjoyed hearing. However, I got distracted from doing this quite early in my efforts. As I contemplated taking on the task of doing this effort with *The Devil's Sooty Brother*, I noticed how similar it was to the story *Bearskin*. The structures of the tales were considerably alike. I liked the subtle differences between the two so much that I was torn between which one I wanted to tackle first. After examining them for some time, I had this crazy notion that I could take poetic liberties and merge them into one tale. So, I did!

And as I did, I realized how enriching this act made the final story. No longer hindered by the decision as to which tale to write about, I was now overwhelmed with the new liberty that I granted myself and I looked for other tales with similar themes. As luck would have it, there were quite a few that were about discharged men no longer knowing what to do with themselves, going down into the earth, tackling change head on and experiencing personal transformation as a result. I found a wellspring of them within the Brothers Grimm Folk Tales, all within one form or another. As I did my prospecting for other tales to merge into this new adventure, I looked for common threads between them and continually found them as I read and reread them.

One curious detail that I came across in this effort is how many versions of these Folk Tales actually existed. One tale I researched had over a dozen variations that changed the number of characters, the numbers of items used or the items themselves and what occurred to some of the characters at specific points in the story. Yet the basics of the story remained intact.

This information changed the whole scope of my approach. I realized I could take the same liberties within my merging tales to create better continuity of characters, names, professions, themes and assorted symbols used within them. This changed my direction dramatically in that I was no longer merely merging these tales; I ultimately used them as building blocks to create an entirely different and more in depth tale. In doing so, I worked toward creating one that was both entertaining in many different ways and conveyed a much larger scope of relevance for those experiencing them.

As I merged the tales, I made every effort to integrate aspects of the masculine archetypes into the overall project by picking and choosing stories that had one or two types already within them. It was clearly evident that there were the four types spoken of within the book, *King Warrior Magician Lover*, of which I used to guide my efforts. It was also clear that I had the Warriors well covered, with both the dark and light sides presented. I identified and incorporated others that brought into the overall tale aspects of the other three.

Interestingly enough, there are aspects of Feminine Archetypes included in these tales. One friend made note of this in a previewed version I shared with him. It led to a long discussion on how each gender had to mature both their masculine and feminine aspects to mature fully as human beings. Even though this was not my focus, it was clear that they did make their presence known in the eventual finished product. That was a delightful surprise!

After putting this tale together, it came to light that there were many different aspects of maturing to which these tales did allude. Coming to maturity requires so many aspects of every person to be developed that the story could become the basis of some serious coursework and study. This is partly the reason behind its creation. Each of the stories within the tale has many themes that can be explored. Some of those themes stand alone. Others intertwine, connecting and supporting the overall tale. Still some of these themes allude to things, issues and conditions that are universal to all tales and in return, to the human condition we all have opportunity from which to learn. To explore them all would take some time, but such an investment would surely benefit those who did.

It is hoped that you first and foremost enjoy how the tale wanders, twists and turns as it unfolds. Should you desire to explore the themes of each section, I have end-noted each with at least one point and question to ponder and explore. I highly recommend though that you read the entire tale first and merely enjoy it as an entertaining and diversionary story. This way you won't interrupt the pleasure of its first meeting with you.

If after you read it through and you want to use the tale to explore deeper themes, I invite you to invest yourself in what is offered within the end-note section.

Above all, enjoy the Journey!

Dr. John S. Nagy

Journey Map

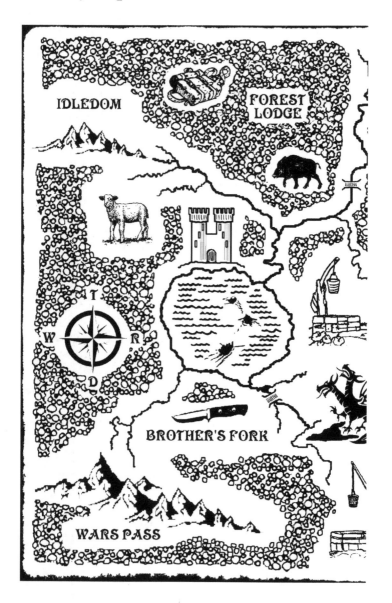

DEVIL'S WAY

BOAR'S RUN

KINGDOMCOME

HELL'S HOLE

HUMBLETON

ENCHANTED FOREST

There was once upon a time a young lad who loved hearing stories.

The more he heard them voiced, the more of them he wanted to hear. As he grew, he became enchanted by each of them and he soon fell deeply under their collective spell.

Spellbound, the lad was compelled to travel within their many realms, and gathered he did up into his knapsack each tale as he went. He traveled and collected them wherever he found himself and

no matter what bourne[a] the lad crossed, their voices sang out to him for capture.

In time the lad grew to manhood and he traveled far and wide. He gathered his tales and soon had so many that some sang in harmony with each other. This delighted him to no end and he made great effort to share what he heard with other travelers he met along his way. Soon many others heard their song too and they beseeched him to share more with them, which the traveler did and gladly so.

As his years mounted in number, he began to listen more carefully to the many voices entwining within his knapsack and as he did, the lad now man noticed some tales sung more in harmony with some than with others and this piqued his curiosity.

He soon found himself forest deep and in a round of trees where there stood upright a lodge to rest himself and his quarry. The traveler entered, made suitable requests of the lodge-keeper and sat down, pulling out each tale that sang best with each other and which tales would best agree.

Ten tales did the grown lad choose in his diligent and earnest efforts. When he pulled them out in total, the traveler noticed they had emerged as one wonder-filled chorus, humming and chanting in most masterfully deep undertones. The lodge resounded with their song and all were moved.

---

[a] Boundary, limit

Roll-Call

There was *Brother Lustig* who was a most unusual Fellow. Generous yet needy, with questionable integrity, he found opportunity all around him yet squandered all benefits without thought. His was a tale of many unforeseen twists and turns.

And then there were *The Two Brothers* who were as genuine as the gold they awoke to each morning. They mastered their profession, were loyal to each other and their paths and came to enjoy the fruits of their labor.

Sadly, there was a poor trusting brother who eventually became *The Singing Bone*, who deserved his day in court and it was with the aid of our Fellow that a pious master would save the day and in more than one way.

It was clear too that vengeance played out its ugly heart when *The Blue Light* brought forth an unquestioning servant for which a hurting and slighted mercenary in attendance did order his dark desires.

And there were, wandering without direction, *The Three Apprentices* eventually, consistently and dutifully parroted what the dark man asked of them, never wavering for a moment from the script they were handed for fear they would lose it all no matter what they did.

Yet, *The Shoes That Were Danced to Pieces* was a mystery to behold and only the well-guided soldier of old in this group could let the emperor know what was afoot.

Then there was *The Gnome* who let the huntsmen have it. But one demanded more and he was rightfully rewarded with a quest requiring him to descend in service.

Then there were *Bearskin* and *The Devil's Sooty Brother* who both did shared some common threads and grief. Their growth was through service that brought them each to far better selves. The riches they reaped for their efforts were immeasurable.

And finally, present was patient *King Thrushbeard* who had more love than could possibly be contained. His purposefully staged steps nurtured his love to grow and to eventually embrace all he had to offer.

The Quilling

To the traveler's delight, they each came forth into the light of his forest lodge with an enchanting tale to tell, with lessons of victory and  defeat, love and loss, growth and decay. He knew the moment they had revealed themselves to him that he was honor bound, nay, obligated to share them with the world.

So, put quill to parchment did he to assume the task of faithfully immortalizing their spirited song as sung for all the world to hear.

Unfolding

And it came to pass that his inked parchment was soon discovered by seekers of light and used thereafter to enchant those who would embrace its song. *Gatherings of Men* great and small came together to listen to its unifying voices and great discourse did ensue upon its many offered lessons.

And in these rounds, truth was uncovered in its many varied forms[b]. Tyranny and subjection did come to rest in the realm, bullies and cowards found peaceful accord on all battlefields, tricksters and fools magically learned together and mama's boys and dreamers found loving balance.

But there were a select masterful few, who themselves had long traveled into the world of letter and number, who have previously laid strong foundations of heart and mind and who had learned well the disciplines of life. In their gatherings divine beings did come forth to embrace their rightful thrones, heroes rescued their lives, precocious souls performed miracles and the hearts of all were opened to the vastness of true fruition.

And this was only the beginning...

---

[b] King, Warrior, Magician, Lover

Table of Contents

Acknowledgements i

Introduction ii

Journey Map viii

Prelude x

Unfolding xiv

   Ye Grand Undertaking 16

   Ye Boaring Death 31

   Ye Forest Ways 47

   Ye Tale Well Worn 65

   Ye Going Down 84

   Ye Dinner Guests 95

   Ye Inn Crowd 106

   Ye Gathering 114

   Ye Shrewed Awakening 121

Appendices 139

   A. Journeyman 139

   B. Journey Flow Chart 140

   C. Bibliography and Resources 142

   D. About the Author 143

   E. Lessons, Points & Fodder to Ponder 144

Ye^c Grand Undertaking

The Old Relic[1]

There was once upon a time an old relic who had mastered the magical gift of tale. He was often called upon by kings, warriors, magicians and lovers to tell his wonder-filled yarns well into the morn.

It was said by those who heard them that his stories were capture by him in his travels, and no one knew for sure if this was true or how it was done.

What was known of him was that his stories enchanted even the most unyielding listeners and he pulled them into his world without woe.

A Dismissal[2]

Early in his life there was a great project, and when it came to an end, many craftsmen were

---

[c] [Archaic] The; [from M.E. þe, (using the letter thorn).]

discharged from its service. It was then that the journeyman Brother Lustig[d] also received his dismissal, and besides that, nothing more than a small loaf of contract-bread, and four silver coins in money, with which he departed.

A pious master called, "Achim[e]", had however placed himself in the discharged journeyman's way in the guise of a poor beggar, and when the journeyman came upon him, he begged alms of him.

The Destitute[3]

The journeyman replied, "Dear beggar-man, what am I to give you? I have been a journeyman, and have received my dismissal. I have nothing but this little loaf of contract-

---

[d] Lustig: [German origin] means "Funny; humorous; enjoyable"

[e] Achim: [German origin] means "One whom God exalts"

bread, and four silver coins of specie[f]. When that is gone, I shall have to beg as well as you. Still I will give you something."

Thereupon he divided the loaf into four parts, and gave the beggar-man one of them, and a silver coin likewise.

The pious master thanked him, went onwards, and threw himself again in the journeyman's way as a beggar, but in another guise. And when Brother Lustig came upon him, he begged a gift of him as before.

The journeyman spoke as he had done before, and again gave him a quarter of the loaf and one silver coin.

Achim thanked him again, and went onwards. But for the third time, he placed himself in another guise as a beggar on his road, and spoke to the discharged journeyman. Brother Lustig gave him also the third quarter of bread and the third silver coin as well

The pious master thanked him for the third time, and the journeyman went onwards, having left but a quarter of the loaf, and one silver coin.

Some Self-Care[4]

With that he went into an inn, ate the bread, and ordered one silver coin's worth of beer.

When he finished his brew, he traveled onwards.

Then Achim, who by then had assumed the similar appearance of a discharged journeyman,

---

[f] Money, especially precious metal coins

met and spoke to him thus: "Good day, fellow, can you not give me a bit of bread, and a silver coin to get a drink?"

"Where am I to procure it?" answered Brother Lustig; "I have been discharged too, and I got nothing but a loaf of contract-bread and four silver coins in money. I too am destitute for I met three beggars on the road, and I gave each of them a quarter of my bread, and one silver coin. The last quarter I ate in the inn, and had a drink with my very last coin. Now my pockets are empty, and as you also have nothing, now we can go a-begging together."

"No," answered the pious master, "we need not quite do that. I know a little about healing, and I shall soon earn as much as I require by that."

"Indeed," said Brother Lustig, "I know nothing of that, so I must then go and beg alone."

"Just come with me," said Achim, "and if I earn anything, you shall have half of it."

"Very well," said the journeyman, so they went onward together.

The Old Man[5]

As fortune would have it, the two travelers soon came to a peasant's house inside which they heard loud lamentations and cries; so they went in. Therein was the husband lying sick unto death, and very near his end. His wife was wailing and weeping quite woefully.

"Stop that horrendous howling," snapped Achim, "I will make your man well again," and he took out a salve from his pocket, and healed the sick man in a moment.

Relieved of his ill burden, the man soon rose up, and was in perfect health.

In great delight the husband and wife rejoiced together, "How can we reward you? What shall we give you?"

But the pious master would take nothing from them, and the more the peasant folks offered him, the more he refused.

The journeyman, however, nudged Achim, and said, "Take something; sure enough we are in great need of it."

At length the woman brought to the two a white lamb and said to the pious master that he really must take that, but he would not.

Then the journeyman gave him a poke in the side, and said, "Do take it, you stupid fool; our stomachs ache and we are in great want of it!"

Then Achim said at last, "Very well. I will take the lamb, but I won't carry it. For your insistence, you must carry it for us."

"That is nothing," boasted the journeyman. "I will easily carry it," and took it upon his shoulder, gleeful that his efforts paid off.

The Lamb's Burden[6]

Then they departed and came to a wood, but the journeyman had begun to feel the lamb's weight, and being filled with hunger he said to Achim, "Look, that's a good place, we might cook the lamb there, and eat it."

"As you like,"
answered the pious
master, "but I can't have
anything to do with the
cooking; if you will cook,
there is a clay kettle for
you, and in the
meantime I will walk
about a little until it is
ready. You must,

however, not begin to eat until I have come back, I
will come at the right time."

"Well, go then," grumbled Brother Lustig, "I
understand cookery, I will manage it well enough
without you."

Then Achim went away, and the journeyman
slew the white lamb, discarding its skin to the side.
He ignited a fire, threw its meat into the kettle, and
boiled it.

The lamb was, however, quickly ready, and the
pious master had not come back. So the
journeyman took it out of the kettle, cut it up, and
found the heart.

"That is said to be the best part," said he, and
tasted a bit of it, but at last he ate it all up.

A Heartless Encounter[7]

At length Achim returned and said the
journeyman, "You may eat the whole of the lamb
yourself. I will only have the heart, give me that."

Then the journeyman took a knife and fork, and
pretended to look anxiously about amongst the

lamb's flesh, but unable to find the heart. At last he said abruptly, "There is none here."

"But where can it be?" said Achim.

"I don't know," replied the journeyman feigning innocence. "But look," he continued, trying to divert the master's attention, "what fools we both are, to seek for the lamb's heart, and neither of us to remember that a lamb has no heart!"

"Oh," said the other, "that is something quite new! Every animal has a heart, why is a lamb to have none?"

"No, be assured, my brother," proclaimed the journeyman with shameless confidence, "that a lamb has no heart; just consider it seriously, and then you will see that it really has none."

"Well, it is all right," said the pious master with quiet reservation, "if there is no heart, then I want none of what you have offered here; you may eat it alone."

"Well enough then. What I can't eat now, I will carry away in my knapsack," said the journeyman, and he ate half the lamb, and put the rest in his knapsack.

The Bourne[8]

They went a traveling farther, and soon thereafter Achim caused a great stream of water to flow right across their path. They were obliged to pass through it.

Asked the pious master, "Do you go first?"

"Nay," answered the journeyman, "begin you," and he thought to himself, "if the water is too deep I will stay safely behind."

Then Achim effortlessly strode through it as the water just reached to his knee. So the journeyman began to go through also, but the water grew deeper with every step and at length it reached his belly and he began to struggle.

Then he cried, "Good brother, help me!"

The pious master said, "Then will you confess that you have eaten the lamb's heart?"

"No," said he without reservation, "I could not have eaten it."

Then the water grew deeper still and rose to his chest.

"Help me, good brother," begged the journeyman.

Achim said, "Then will you confess that you have eaten the lamb's heart?"

"No," he replied indignantly, "I have not eaten it."

Then the water grew deeper still and rose to his throat.

"Help me, good brother, I fear I am near death" wailed Brother Lustig.

The pious master said, "Then will you confess that you have eaten the lamb's heart?"

"No," he shouting near pain, "I did not eat it."

Achim did not believe him, however, would not knowingly let any man be drowned, even in the waters of his own making. So he made the water sink and helped the journeyman through it.

A Timely Death[9]

Then the two journeyed onwards, and came to a realm where they heard that Princess Galiana[g], one of three King Ultman[h]'s daughters, lay sick unto death.

"Hollo[i], brother!" said the journeyman to the pious master, "this is a chance for us; if we can heal her we shall be provided for, for life!"

But Achim was not half quick enough for him, "Come, lift your legs, my dear brother," said he impatiently, "that we may get there in time."

But Achim walked slower and slower, though Brother Lustig did all he could to drive and push him onward. At last they heard that the princess was dead.

"Now we are done for!" said the journeyman; "that comes of your sleepy way of walking!"

"Just be quiet," patiently answered the pious master, "I can do more than cure sick people. I can bring dead ones to life again."

"Well, if you can do that," said Brother Lustig, "it's all right then. But you should earn at least half the realm for us by that."

They soon arrived at the royal palace, where everyone was in great grief. But the pious master told King Ultman that he would restore his precious daughter to life. The king was beside himself with despair and took his offer with great hope.

---

[g] Galiana: [German origin] means "Haughty"
[h] Ultman: [German origin] means "Noble Stone"
[i] Hollo: a cry for attention, or of encouragement

Achim was quickly taken to her body, and said, "Bring me a clay kettle, charcoal, limestone and some water," and when these were brought, he bade[j] everyone go out, and allowed no one to remain with him but the journeyman.

Then he cut off all the dead princess' limbs, and threw them in the clay kettle's water, lighted a limestone encircled charcoal fire beneath it, and boiled them. And when the flesh had cleaved from the bones, he grasped the beautiful white bones, raised them out of the clay kettle, and laid them upon a table, arranging them together in their natural order.

When he had done that, he stepped forward and said three times, "In the name of the most high, dead woman, arise." And at the third time, the princess arose, living, healthy, whole and beautiful once more.

Then the king was in the greatest joy. He said to Achim, "Ask for your reward; even if it were half my realm, I would give it you."

But the pious master said, "I want for nothing."

"Oh, you tomfool!" thought the journeyman to himself, and nudged his comrade's side, and said, "Don't be so stupid! If you have no need of anything, I have."

Achim, however, would have nothing, but as King Ultman saw that the other would very much like to have something, he ordered his treasurer to fill the journeyman's knapsack with gold.

---

[j] Bade: commanded; ordered; directed

A Golden Divide[10]

Then they went on their way, and when they came to a nearby forest, the pious master said to Brother Lustig, "Now, we will divide the gold."

"Yes," he replied, "we will."

So Achim divided the gold, and divided it into three heaps as he did.

The journeyman thought to himself, "What craze has he got in his head now? He is making three shares, and there are but two of us!"

The dividing now done, the pious master said, "I have divided it exactly; there is one share for me, one for you, and one for him who ate the lamb's heart."

"Oh, I ate that!" replied the journeyman without a second thought, and hastily swept up the gold to his pocket. "You may trust what I say."

"But how can that be true," said Achim, "when you gave unto me your word that a lamb has no heart?"

"Eh, what, brother, what can you be thinking of? Lambs have hearts like other animals, why should only they have none?"

The pious master saw the journeyman's severed nature and knew he had lost his tongue to falsehood. "Well, so be it," said Achim. "Keep the gold to yourself. I will stay with you no longer and go my way alone".

"As you like, dear brother," answered the journeyman. "Farewell."

Then the pious master went to different roads, and Brother Lustig thought, "It is a good thing that he has taken himself off, he is certainly a strange sort, after all."

Then he had money enough, but did not know how to manage it. He squandered it, gave it away, and when some time had gone by, once more had nothing.

The Brother's Twins[11]

There were also at this time in a nearby town two brothers, one rich and the other poor. The rich one, Bernal[k], was a goldsmith and evil-hearted. The poor one, Gilardo[l], supported himself by making brooms, and was good and honorable. The poor one had two children, who were twin brothers and as like each other as two drops of water. The two boys, Odwin[m] and Baldwyn[n], went backwards and forwards to the rich Uncle's house, and often got some of the scraps to eat.

It happened once when the poor man was going into the forest to fetch brush-wood, that he saw a bird which was quite golden and more beautiful than any he had ever chanced to meet with. He picked up a small stone, threw it at him, and was lucky enough to hit him. As one golden feather fell down the bird flew away.

Gilardo took the feather and carried it to his brother, who looked at it and said, "It is pure gold!"

---

[k] Bernal: [German origin] means "Strong as a bear"
[l] Gilardo: [German origin] means "Good"
[m] Odwin: [German origin] means "Noble Friend"
[n] Baldwyn: [German origin] means "Bold-Brave Friend"

and gave him a great deal of money for it.

Next day the man climbed into a birch-tree, and was about to cut off a couple of branches when the same bird flew out, and when the man searched he found a nest, and an egg lay inside it, which was of gold.

He took the egg home with him, and carried it to his brother, who again said, "It is pure gold," and gave him what it was worth. At last the goldsmith said, "I should indeed like to have the bird itself."

The poor man went into the forest for the third time, and again saw the golden bird sitting on the tree, so he took a stone and brought it down and carried it to his brother, who gave him a great heap of gold for it.

"Now I can get on," thought Gilardo, and he went contentedly home.

Bernal however was crafty and cunning, and knew very well what kind of a bird it was. He called his wife and said, "Roast me the gold bird, and take care that none of it is lost. I have a fancy to eat it all myself."

The bird, however, was no common one, but of so wondrous a kind that whosoever ate its heart or liver found every morning a piece of gold beneath his pillow.

The woman made the bird ready, put it on the spit, and let it roast.

A Roast[12]

Now it happened that while it was at the fire, and the woman was forced to go out of the kitchen on account of some other work, the two children of the poor broom-maker ran in, stood by the spit and turned it round once or twice. And as at that very moment two little bits of the bird fell down into the dripping-tin, Baldwyn said, "We will eat these two little bits; I am so hungry, and no one will ever miss them."

Then the two ate the pieces, but the woman came into the kitchen and saw that they were eating something and said, "What have ye been eating?"

"Two little morsels which fell out of the bird," answered they.

"That must have been the heart and the liver," said the woman, quite frightened. In order that her husband might not miss them and be angry, she quickly killed a young cock, took out his heart and liver, and put them beside the golden bird. When it was ready, she carried it to the goldsmith, who consumed it all alone, and left none of it.

Next morning, however, when he felt beneath his pillow, and expected to bring out the piece of gold, no more gold pieces were there now than there had always been before.

The two children did not know what a piece of good-fortune had fallen to their lot. Next morning when they arose, something fell rattling to the ground, and when they picked it up there were two gold pieces!

They took them to their father, who was astonished and said, "How can that have happened?"

When next morning they again found two, and so on daily, he went to his brother and told him the strange story. The goldsmith at once knew how it had come to pass, and that the children had eaten the heart and liver of the golden bird. In order to revenge himself, and because he was envious and hard-hearted, he said to the father, "Thy children are in league with the Evil One, do not take the gold, and do not suffer them to stay any longer in your house, for he has them in his power, and may ruin you likewise."

The father feared the Evil One, and painful as it was to him, he nevertheless led the twins forth into the forest, and with a sad heart left them there.

A Chance Encounter[13]

And now the two children ran about the forest, and sought the way home again, but could not find it, and only lost themselves more and more.

At length they met with a huntsman called, "Keane°", who asked, "To whom do you children belong?"

"We are the poor broom-maker's boys," they replied, and they told him that their father would not keep them any longer in the house because a piece of gold lay every morning under their pillows.

"Come," said the huntsman, "that is nothing so very bad, if at the same time you keep honest, and are not idle."

As the good man liked the children, and had none of his own, he took them home with him and said, "I will father you, and raise you up till you can stand as men."

° Keane: [German origin] means "Bold; Sharp"

The twins learnt the ways of the hunt from him, and the piece of gold which each of them found when he awoke, was kept for them by him in case they should be in need in the future.

Ye Boaring Death

A Fortunate Encounter[14]

In the meantime, the people of a nearby country had great lamentation over a wild boar that laid waste the farmer's fields, killed the cattle, and ripped up people's bodies with his tusks. King Oderico[p], the monarch of the land, promised a large reward to anyone who would free the land from this plague; but the beast was so big

---

[p] Oderico: [German origin] means "Powerful in riches"

and strong that no one dared to go near the forest in which it lived.

At last the monarch gave notice that whosoever should capture or kill the wild boar shall have his only daughter to wife.

Now there lived in the country two unskilled but willing brothers, sons of a poor man, who declared themselves willing to undertake the hazardous and important undertaking. Barnett[q], the elder, was crafty and shrewd out of pride. Sterlyn[r], the younger, was innocent and simple from a kind heart.

King Oderico said, "In order that you may be the more sure of finding the beast, you must go into the forest from opposite sides." So the elder went in on the west side, and the younger entered in on the east.

When the younger had gone a short way, a little man stepped up to him. He held in his hand a black spear and said, "I am Garvyn[s] and I give you this spear because your heart is pure and good. With this you can boldly attack the wild boar and it will do you no harm."

Sterlyn thanked the little man, shouldered the spear, and went on fearing no danger.

---

[q] Barnett: [German origin] means "Bear-like"
[r] Sterlyn: [German origin] means "Of high-quality; Pure; Easterner"
[s] Garvyn: [German origin] means "Spear Friend; Ally"

The Beast[15]

Before long he saw the beast, which rushed at him. But he held the spear towards it, and in its blind fury it ran so swiftly against it that its chest was ripped open and its heart was severed in twain.

With the monster put to rest, he took it on his back and went homewards to the monarch.

As he came out at the western side of the wood, there stood at the entrance a house where people were making merry with wine and dancing. His elder brother had gone in here, and, thinking that after all, the boar would not run away from him, was going to drink himself brave.

But when he saw his young brother coming out of the wood laden with his booty, his envious, evil heart gave him no peace. Barnett called out to him, "Come in, dear brother, rest and refresh yourself with a cup of wine." The young hero, who

suspected no evil, went in and told him about the good little man who had given him the spear wherewith he had slain the boar.

The elder brother kept him there until long into the night, and then they went away together. When out in the darkness of night for some time, they came to a bridge which crossed over a brook. Barnett let his brother go first and when he was half-way across he gave him such a blow to his head that the young brother fell down dead.

The murderer buried his brother beneath the bridge and at water's edge. He took the boar for his own, and carried it to the monarch, pretending that he had killed it; whereupon he obtained the monarch's daughter for marriage.

And when his younger brother did not come back he said, "The boar must have killed him," and every one was none the wiser.

A Shepherd's Overlook[16]

But as nothing remains hidden under the canopy of heaven, so too was this dark deed to come to light.

Not long afterwards, a shepherd was driving his herd across the bridge, and spied lying in the sand beneath, a snow-white little bone. He thought that it would make a good flute, so he clambered down the bank, picked it up, and fashioned it all to play.

But when he blew through it for the first time, to his great astonishment, the bone began to sing of its own accord:

"My friend, you blow through my core!
Too long have I lain beside the water.

My brother slew me for the boar,
And took for his wife the monarch's young
daughter."

"What a wonderful flute!" said the shepherd; "it sings by itself; I must take it to my lord the monarch."

And when he came with it to King Oderico, the flute again began to sing its little song. The monarch understood it all, and caused the riverbank below the bridge to be dug up. Soon the remaining skeleton of the murdered brother came to light.

The wicked brother could no longer deny the evil deed. By order of the monarch, Barnett was branded a murderer, commanded to dig his own grave by the water's edge and to lie within its cold damp embrace until death took its toll.

Rough Edges[17]

As luck would have it, the journeyman traveled into this monarch's country and heard that the bones of a hero were recently discovered.

"Oh, ho!" thought Brother Lustig, "that may be a good thing for me; I will bring him to life again, and see that I am paid as I ought to be."

So he went to King Oderico, and offered to raise this dead hero to life again.

Now the monarch had heard that a discharged journeyman was traveling about and bringing dead persons to life again, and thought that the journeyman was this man; but as he had no confidence in him, he consulted his councilors first, who said that he might give it a trial as this brother was certainly dead.

Then the journeyman ordered water to be brought to him in a clay kettle, bade every one go out, cleaned the bones thoroughly, threw them in the water and lighted a limestone encircled charcoal fire beneath it, just as he had seen the pious master do.

The water began to boil, and the bones cleaned up well. Then he took the bones out and laid them on the table, but he did not know the order in which to lay them, and placed them all wrong and in confusion.

Then he stood before them and said, "In the name of the most high, dead brother, I bid thee arise," and he said this thrice, but the bones did stir not.

So he said it thrice more, but also in vain: "Confounded boy that you are, get up!" cried he, "Get up, or it shall be worse for you!"

A Masterful Entrance[18]

When he had said that, Achim, who had bid him farewell, suddenly appeared in his former shape as a discharged journeyman; he entered by the window and said, "Godless man! What in heaven's name are you doing? How can this dead man rise, when you have thrown about his bones in such confusion?"

"Dear brother, I have done everything to the best of my ability," he responded.

"This once, I will help you out of your difficulty. But I demand of you in return, that you never undertake anything of this greatness or importance again and also that you must neither demand nor accept the smallest thing from the monarch for this! It will be the worse for you if you do."

"Aye, agreed" said the journeyman grateful for his deliverance.

Thereupon Achim laid all the brother's bones in their right order, including the one fashioned to flute. He said to the brother's bones three times, "In the name of the most high, dead brother, arise," and on the third time, Sterlyn arose, healthy, whole and as lively as before.

Then the pious master went away again by the window, and the journeyman was rejoiced to find that all had passed off so well, but was very much vexed to think that after all he was not to take anything for it.

"I should just like to know," thought he, "what fancy that fellow has got in his head, for what he gives with one hand he takes away with the other. There is no sense whatever in it!"

Then King Oderico, knowing no better, offered the journeyman whatsoever he wished to have, but he did not dare to ask or take anything. However, by devious cues, purposeful equivocation and shrewd cunning, he slyly contrived to make the monarch order his knapsack to be filled with gold for him, and with that he departed.

The revived young hero however soon took his rightful place as husband to the princess.

The **Sacked Journeyman**[19]

Soon thereafter the journeyman traveled a short distance and out of King Ultman's realm. The pious master reappeared along his path, and said, "Just look what a man you are! Did I not demand you to take nothing, and there you have your knapsack full of gold!"

"I asked for nothing to be put in my sack to take" protested Brother Lustig, "How can I help that, if people will put things in for me?"

"Well, I tell you this, that if ever you set about anything of this kind again you shall suffer greatly for it!"

"Eh, brother, have no fear, now I have money, why should I trouble myself with washing bones?"

"Faith," said Achim, "the gold will last a long time! In order that after this you may never tread in forbidden paths, I will bestow on your knapsack this property, namely, that whatsoever you wish to have inside it shall be there. Farewell, you shall now see me take my leave of you."

"Good-bye," said the journeyman, and thought to himself, "I am very glad that you have taken yourself off, you strange fellow; I shall certainly not follow you."

But of the magical power which had been bestowed on his knapsack, he thought no more.

Twin Masteries[20]

It was at this time that twin Brothers Odwin and Baldwyn came of age, and their foster-father, Keane, took them into the forest with him and said, "To-day shall you make your trial shot, so that I may release you from your apprenticeship, and make you free huntsmen."

They went with him to lie in wait and stayed there a long time, but no game appeared. The huntsman, however, looked above him and saw a covey of wild geese flying in the form of a triangle, and said to one of them, "Shoot me down one from each corner."

He did it, and thus accomplished his trial shot.

Soon after another covey came flying by in the form of the figure two, and the huntsman bade the other also bring down one from each corner, and his trial shot was likewise successful.

"Now," said the foster-father, "I pronounce you out of your apprenticeship; you are skilled huntsmen and free to travel."

The Plan[21]

Thereupon the two brothers went forth together into the forest, and took counsel with each other and planned something. And in the evening when they had sat down to supper, they said to their foster-father, "We will not touch food, or take one mouthful, until you have granted us a request."

Said he, "What, then, is your request?"

They replied, "We have now finished learning, and we must prove ourselves in the world, so allow us to go away and travel."

Then spake the old man joyfully, "You talk like brave and true huntsmen, that which you desire has been my wish; go forth, all will go well with you."

Thereupon they ate and drank joyously together.

A Sharp Instrument[22]

When the appointed day came, their foster-father presented each of them with a good gun and his blessings, and let each of them take as many of his saved-up gold pieces as each chose.

Then Keane accompanied them a part of the way, and when taking leave, he gave them a bright knife, and said, "If ever you separate, stick this knife into a tree at the place where you part, and when one of you goes back, he will be able to see how his absent brother is faring, for the side of the knife which is turned in the direction by which he went, will rust if he dies, but will remain bright as long as he is alive."

And with that, the huntsman gave them his blessings and went his separate way.

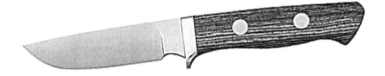

The Mission[23]

There was also at this time a mercenary called, "Helmer[t]", who for many years had served a tyrant faithfully, but when the war came to an end could serve no longer because of the many wounds which he had received. The tyrant said to him: "You may return to your home, I need you no longer, and you

---

[t] Helmer: [German origin] means "Wrath of a warrior"

will not receive any more money, for he only receives wages who renders me service for them."

The mercenary did not know how to earn a living and went away greatly troubled. He walked the whole day, until in the evening he entered a forest.

When darkness came on, Helmer saw a light, which he went up to, and came to a house wherein lived an old woman named "Grieselda[u]".

"Do give me one night's lodging, and a little to eat and drink," said he to her, "or I shall starve."

"Oho!" she answered, "who gives anything to a run-away mercenary? Yet will I be compassionate, and take you in, if you will do what I wish."

"What do you wish?" said the mercenary.

"That you should dig all round my garden for me, tomorrow."

Helmer consented and next day labored with all his strength, but could not finish it by the

---

[u] Grieselda: [German origin] means ""dark battle" or "gravel; stone" or "Grey maiden warrior""

evening.

"I see well enough," said the crone, "that you can do no more today, but I will keep you yet another night, in payment for which you must tomorrow chop me a load of wood, and chop it small."

The mercenary spent the whole day in doing it, and in the evening Grieselda proposed that he should stay one night more.

"Tomorrow, you shall only do me a very trifling piece of work. Behind my house, there is an old dry well, into which my light has fallen, it burns blue, and never goes out, and you shall bring it up again."

A Retrieval[24]

Next day the old woman took Helmer to the well, and let him down in a basket. He found the blue light, and made her a signal to draw him up again. She did draw him up, but when he came near the edge, Grieselda stretched down her hand wanting to take the blue light away from him.

"No," said he, perceiving her evil intention, "I will not give you the light until I am standing with both feet upon the ground."

The old crone fell into a passion, let him fall again into the well, and went away.

The poor mercenary fell without injury onto the moist ground, and the blue light went on burning, but of what use was that to him? Helmer saw very well that he could not escape death. He sat for a while very sorrowfully, thinking the shortness of his days. Suddenly he felt in his pocket and found his flute, which was still in good repair.

"This shall be my last pleasure," thought he, pulled it out, sat down at the blue light and began to play.

When its sound echoed about the cavern, suddenly a gnome stood before him, and said: "Lord, what are your commands?"

"What my commands are?" replied Helmer, quite astonished.

"I must do everything you bid me," said the little man.

"Good," said the mercenary; "then in the first place help me out of this well."

The gnome took Helmer by the hand, and led him through an underground passage, but the mercenary did not forget to take the blue light with him. On the way the little man showed him the treasures and stone statues which the crone had created, collected and hidden there, and Helmer took as much gold as he could carry.

When he was above, he said to the gnome: "Now go, dispatch the old witch from these parts, and drive her to the deepest forest."

In a short time she came by like the wind, riding on a wild tom-cat and screaming frightfully. Nor was it long before the gnome reappeared. "It is all done," said he, "and the old witch is already deep in the forest, grazing as a snow-white hart[v] to mask her appearance.

What further commands has my lord?" inquired the gnome.

"At this moment, none," answered the mercenary; "you may return home, only be at hand immediately, when I summon you."

"Nothing more is needed than that you should play your flute at the blue light, and I will appear before you at once."

Thereupon he vanished from Helmer's sight.

Further Travels[25]

In the meantime, Brother Lustig travelled about with his money, and squandered and wasted what he had as before. When at last he had no more than four silver coins, he passed by an inn and thought, "The money must go," and ordered three silver coins' worth of wine and one silver coin's worth of bread for himself.

As he was sitting there drinking, the smell of roast goose made its way to his nose. The journeyman looked about and peeped, and saw that the host had two geese roasting in the oven. Then he remembered that his comrade had said that whatsoever he wished to have in his knapsack should be there, so he said, "Oh, ho! I must try that with the geese."

---

[v] Hart: an adult male deer, esp. one over five years old.

So he went out, and when he was outside the door, he said, "I wish those two roasted geese out of the oven and in my knapsack." And when he had said that, he unbuckled it and looked in, and to his delight, there they were inside it.

"Ah, that's right!" said he, "now I am a made man!" and he went away to a meadow and took out the roast meat.

The Journeymen[26]

When the journeyman was in the midst of his meal, two other journeymen came up and looked with hungry eyes at the second goose, which was not yet touched. Brother Lustig thought to himself, "One is enough for me," and called the two men over and said, "Take the goose, and eat it to my health."

They thanked him, and went with it to the inn, ordered themselves a half bottle of wine and a loaf, took out the roasted goose which had been given them, and began to eat. The hostess saw them and said to her husband, "Those two are eating a goose; just look and see if it is not one of ours, out of the oven."

The landlord ran thither, and behold the oven was empty!

"What!" cried he, "you thievish crew, you want to eat goose as cheap as that? Pay for it this moment; or I will wash you well with green hazel-sap."

The two said, "We are no thieves, a discharged journeyman gave us the goose, outside there in the meadow."

"You shall not throw dust in my eyes that way! The journeyman was here but he went out by the door, like an honest fellow. I looked after him myself. You are the thieves and shall pay!"

But as they could not pay, he took a stick, and cudgeled[w] them out of the house.

---

[w] Cudgeled: To beat with a cudgel; bludgeon, club, beat, batter, bash

Ye Forest Ways

A Deeper Path[27]

During this time, the two twin brothers had traveled long, and in time they came to a forest which was so large that it was impossible for them to get out of it in one day. So they passed the night in it, and ate what they had put in their hunting-pouches, but they walked all the second day likewise and still did not get out.

As they had nothing to eat, one of them said, "We must shoot something for ourselves or we shall suffer from hunger," and loaded his gun, and looked about him. And when an old hare came running up towards them, he laiqd his gun on his shoulder, but the hare cried,

"Dear huntsman, do but let me live,
Two little ones I'll likewise give."

And the hare sprang instantly into the thicket, and brought two young ones. But the little creatures played so merrily, and were so pretty, that the huntsmen could not find it in their hearts to kill them. They therefore kept them with them, and the little hares followed on foot.

Soon after this, a fox crept past; they were just going to shoot it, but the fox cried,

"Dear huntsman, do but let me live,
Two little ones I'll likewise give."

He, too, brought two little foxes, and the huntsmen did not like to kill them either, but gave them to the hares for company, and they followed behind.

It was not long before a wolf strode out of the thicket; the huntsmen made ready to shoot him, but the wolf cried,

"Dear huntsman, do but let me live,
Two little ones I'll likewise give."

The huntsmen put the two wolves beside the other animals, and they followed behind them.

Then a bear came who wanted to trot about a little longer, and cried:

"Dear huntsman, do but let me live,
Two little ones I'll likewise give."

The two young bears were added to the others, and there were already eight of them.

At length who came? A lion came, and tossed his mane. But the huntsmen did not let themselves be frightened and aimed at him likewise, but the lion also said,

"Dear huntsman, do but let me live,
Two little ones I'll likewise give."

And he brought his little ones to them, and now the huntsmen had two lions, two bears, two wolves, two foxes, and two hares, who followed them and served them.

The Divide[28]

None of this helped though for their hunger was not appeased at all, and they said to the foxes,

"Hark ye, cunning fellows, provide us with something to eat. You are crafty and deep."

They replied, "Not far from here lies a village, from which we have already brought many a fowl; we will show you the way there."

So, they went into the village, bought themselves something to eat, had some food given to their beasts, and then travelled onwards.

The foxes, however, knew their way very well about the district and where the poultry-yards were, and were able to guide the huntsmen.

Now they travelled about for a while, but could find no situations where they could remain together, so they said, "There is nothing else for it, we must part."

They divided the animals, so that each of them had a lion, a bear, a wolf, a fox, and a hare, then they took leave of each other, promised to love each other as brothers till their death, and stuck the knife which their foster-father had given them, into a tree, after which one went east, and the other went west.

The Castle[29]

Meanwhile, Brother Lustig went his way and came to a place where there was a magnificent castle, and not far from it a wretched inn. He went to the inn and asked for a night's lodging, but the landlord turned him away, and said, "There is no more room here; the house is full of noble guests."

"It surprises me that they should come to you and not go to that splendid castle," said the journeyman.

"Ah, indeed," replied the innkeeper, "but it is no slight matter to sleep there for a night; no one who has tried it so far, has ever come out of it alive."

"If others have tried it," said the journeyman, "I will try it too."

"Leave it alone," cautioned the host, "it will cost you your neck."

"It won't kill me at once," quipped Brother Lustig, "just give me the key, and some good food and wine."

So the innkeeper gave him the key, and food and wine as well. With this the journeyman plied the key to the door, went into the castle and enjoyed his supper. At length, as he was sleepy, he lay down on the ground, for there was no bed.

The Devil You Say[30]

He soon fell asleep, but during the night was disturbed by a great noise, and when he awoke, the journeyman saw seven ugly shadows in the room, who had made a tight circle, and were dancing around him.

The journeyman said, "Well, dance as long as you like, but none of you must come too close."

But the shadows pressed continually nearer and nearer to him, and almost stepped on his face with their hideous feet.

"Stop, you devils' ghosts," insisted he, but they behaved still worse.

Then the journeyman grew angry, and cried, "Very Well! I will soon make it quiet," and got the leg of a chair and struck out into the midst of them with it.

But seven shadows against one journeyman were still too many, and when he struck those in front of him, the others seized him from behind by the hair, and tore it unmercifully.

"Devils' crew," cried he, "it is getting too bad, but wait!" he recalled, "Into my knapsack, the seven of you!"

In an instant they were in it. He buckled it up and threw it to a corner.

After this, all was quiet with all but the shadows' echo sounding deep into the castle halls. The journeyman lay down again, and slept till it was bright day.

Getting Hammered[31]

Then came the innkeeper, and the nobleman to whom the castle belonged, to see how he had fared. But when they perceived that he was merry and well they were astonished!

They asked, "Have the spirits done you no harm, then?"

"The reason why they have not," answered Brother Lustig, "is because I have got the whole lot of them in my knapsack! You may once more inhabit your castle quite tranquilly; none of them will ever haunt it again."

The nobleman thanked him, made him rich presents, and begged him to remain in his service, saying he would provide for him as long as he lived.

"Nay," replied the journeyman, "by now, I am used to wandering about, I will travel farther."

Then he went away, and entered into a local smithy[x]. He laid the knapsack upon the anvil, which contained the seven shadows, and asked the smith to have his three apprentices strike it long and hard.

So they smote the knapsack with their great gavels and with all their

[x] Smithy: Blacksmith

strength blows did fall. With every strike, the shadows uttered pitiful howls heard above the music of the anvil.

At last, when the hammers last sounded and he opened the knapsack, six of them were turned to dust. But one which had been lying in a fold of it, was still alive, slipped away, and went limping back to hell.

A Duvium[y, 32]

Thereafter, Brother Lustig travelled a long time about the world, and those who know them can tell many a story about him. But as all men who last do, he grew old, and thought of his end. So he came to a hermit who was known to be a prudent man.

The journeyman said to him, "I am tired of wandering about. I have had no aim. I want now to behave in such a manner that I shall enter into the kingdom of Heaven."

The hermit responded, "There are two roads. One is broad and pleasant, and leads to hell. The other is narrow and rough, and leads to heaven."

"I should be a fool," thought the journeyman, "if I were to take any narrow and rough road."

So he set out and took to the broad and pleasant, dusting[z] his path along the way.

---

[y] Duvium: Two-fold path or way
[z] Dusting: Alluding to the six devils he had dusted in his knapsack.

The Burdened Three[33]

Back at the local smithy, the three apprentices were greatly troubled. They had agreed to keep always together while travelling, and always to work in the same town.

At this time, however, their master had failed them and had no more work to give them, so that at last they were in rags, and had nothing to live on.

Finally one of them said, "What shall we do? We cannot stay here any longer, we will travel once more, and if we do not find any work in the town we go to, we will arrange with the lodge-keeper there that we are to write and tell him where we are staying, so that we can always have news of each other, and then we will separate." And that seemed best to the others also.

They went forth, and met on the way a richly-dressed man who asked who they were. "We are apprentices looking for work; Up to this time we have kept together, but if we cannot find anything to do we are going to separate."

"There is no need for that," said the man, "if you will do what I tell you, you shall not want for gold or for work; nay, you shall become great lords, and drive in your carriages!"

One of them said, "If our souls and salvation be not endangered, we will certainly do it."

"They will not," replied the man, "I have no claim on you."

One of the others had, however, looked at his feet, and when he saw a horse's foot and a man's foot, he did not want to have anything to do with him for his very looks betrayed him.

This devil of a man, however, said, "Be easy, I have no designs on you, but on another soul, which is half my own already, and whose measure shall but run full."

As they were now secure, they consented, and the man told them what he wanted.

The first was to answer, "All three of us," to every question; the second was to say, "For money," and the third, "And quite right too!"

They were always to parrot this, one after the other, but they were not to say one word more, and if they disobeyed this order, all their money would disappear at once, but so long as they observed it, their pockets would always be full.

As a beginning, he at once gave them as much as they could carry, and told them to go to such and such a lodge when they got to the village.

The Town[34]

Soon thereafter, in a far off country, Baldwyn, the younger twin brother, arrived with his beasts in a town which was all hung with black crape. He went into an inn, and asked the host if he could accommodate his animals. The innkeeper gave him a stable, where there was a hole in the wall, and the hare crept out and fetched himself the head of a cabbage, and the fox fetched himself a hen, and when he had devoured that got the cock as well, but the wolf, the bear, and the lion could not get out because they were too big.

Then the innkeeper let them be taken to a place where a cow was just then lying on the grass, that they might eat till they were satisfied.

And when the huntsman had taken care of his animals, he asked the innkeeper why the town was thus hung with black crape?

Said the host, "Because King Wilford's[aa] only daughter Tugenda[bb] is to die to-morrow."

Baldwyn inquired if she was "sick unto death?"

"No," answered the host, "she is vigorous and healthy, nevertheless she must die!"

"How is that?" asked the huntsman.

"There is a high hill outside the town, whereon dwells a dragon who every year must have a pure virgin, or he lays the whole country waste, and now all the maidens have already been given to him, and there is no longer anyone left but the King's daughter, yet there is no mercy for her; she must be given up to him, and that is to be done on the morrow."

Said Baldwyn, "Why is the dragon not killed?"

"Ah," replied the host, "so many knights have tried it, but it has cost all of them their lives. The King has promised that he who conquers the dragon shall have his daughter to wife, and shall likewise rule the kingdom after his own death."

[aa] Wilford: [German origin] means "Desires peace"
[bb] Tugenda: [German origin] means "one who is virtuous"

A Sword & Brew[35]

The huntsman said nothing more to this, but next morning took his animals, and with them ascended the dragon's hill. A little church stood at the top of it, and on the altar three full cups were standing, with the inscription, "Whosoever empties the cups will become the strongest man on earth, and will be able to wield the sword which is buried before the threshold of the door."

Baldwyn did not drink, but first went out and sought for the sword in the ground, but was unable to move it from its place. Then he went in and emptied the cups, and now he was strong enough to take up the sword, and

his hand did quite easily wield it.

When the hour came when the maiden was to be delivered over to the dragon, the King, the marshal, and courtiers accompanied her.

From afar Tugenda saw the huntsman on the dragon's hill, and thought it was the dragon standing there waiting for her, and did not want to go up to him, but at last, because otherwise the whole town would have been destroyed, she was forced to go the miserable journey.

The King and courtiers returned home full of grief; the King's marshal, however, was to stand still, and see all from a distance.

When the King's daughter got to the top of the hill, it was not the dragon which stood there, but the young huntsman, who comforted her, and said he would save her. He led her into the church and locked her therein.

The Dragon[36]

It was not long before the seven-headed dragon came thither with loud roaring. When he perceived Baldwyn, he was astonished and said, "What business have you here on the hill?"

The huntsman answered, "I want to fight with you."

Said the dragon, "Many knights have left their lives here, I shall soon have made an end of you too," and he breathed fire out of seven jaws.

The fire was to have lighted the dry grass, and Baldwyn was to have been suffocated in the heat and smoke, but the animals came running up and trampled out the fire.

Then the dragon rushed upon the huntsman, but he swung his sword until it sang through the air, and struck off three of his heads.

Then the dragon grew right furious, and rose up in the air, and spat out flames of fire over Baldwyn, and was about to plunge down on him, but the huntsman once more drew out his sword, and again cut off three of his heads.

The monster became faint and sank down, nevertheless it was just able to rush upon Baldwyn, but he with his last strength smote its tail off, and as he could fight no longer, called up his animals who tore it in pieces.

When the struggle was ended, the huntsman unlocked the church, and found the King's daughter lying on the floor, as she had lost her senses with anguish and terror during the contest.

He carried her out, and when Tugenda came to herself once more, and opened her eyes, he showed her the dragon all cut to pieces, and told her that she was now delivered.

She rejoiced and said, "Now you will be my dearest husband, for my father has promised me to he who kills the dragon."

Thereupon Tugenda took off her necklace of coral, and divided it amongst the animals in order to reward them, and the lion received the golden clasp.

Her pocket-handkerchief, however, on which was her name, she gave to Baldwyn, who went and cut the tongues out of the dragon's seven heads, wrapped them in the handkerchief, and preserved them carefully.

An Assured Rest[37]

That done, as he was so faint and weary with the fire and the battle, he said to the maiden, "We are both faint and weary. We will sleep awhile."

Then Tugenda said, "yes," and they lay down on the ground, and Baldwyn said to the lion, "You shall keep watch, that no one surprises us in our sleep," and both fell asleep.

The lion lay down beside them to watch, but he also was so weary with the fight, that he called to the bear and said, "Lie down near me, I must sleep a little: if anything comes, waken me."

Then the bear lay down beside him, but he also was tired, and called the wolf and said, "Lie down by me, I must sleep a little, but if anything comes, waken me."

Then the wolf lay down by him, but he was tired likewise, and called the fox and said, "Lie down by me, I must sleep a little; if anything comes, waken me."

Then the fox lay down beside him, but he too was weary, and called the hare and said, "Lie down near me, I must sleep a little, and if anything should come, waken me."

Then the hare sat down by him, but the poor hare was tired too, and had no one whom he could call there to keep watch, and fell asleep.

And now the King's daughter, Baldwyn, the lion, the bear, the wolf, the fox, and the hare, were all sleeping a sound sleep.

The Opportunist[38]

The marshal, however, who was to look on from a distance, took courage when he did not see the dragon flying away with the maiden, and finding that all the hill had become quiet, ascended it. There lay the dragon hacked and hewn to pieces on the ground, and not far from it were the King's daughter and a huntsman with his animals, and all of them were sunk in a sound sleep.

And as he was wicked and godless he took his sword, cut off the huntsman's head, and seized the maiden in his arms, and carried her down the hill.

Then she awoke and was terrified, but the marshal said, "You are in my hands, you shall say that it was I who killed the dragon."

"I cannot do that," Tugenda replied, "for it was a huntsman with his animals who did it."

Then he drew his sword, and threatened to kill her if she did not obey him, and so compelled her that she promised it.

Then he took Tugenda to King Wilford, who did not know how to contain himself for joy when he once more looked on his dear child in life, whom he had believed to have been torn to pieces by the monster.

The marshal said to him, "I have killed the dragon, and delivered the maiden and the whole kingdom as

well, therefore I demand her as my wife, as was
promised."

The King said to Tugenda, "Is what he says
true?"

"Ah, yes," she answered, "it must indeed be
true, but I will not consent to have the wedding
celebrated until after a year and a day," for she
thought in that time she should hear something of
her dear huntsman.

A Wakeup Call[39]

The animals, however, were still lying sleeping
beside their dead master on the dragon's hill, and
there came a great humble-bee and lighted on the
hare's nose, but the hare wiped it off with his paw,
and went on sleeping.

The humble-bee came a second time, but the
hare again rubbed it off and slept on.

Then it came for the third time, and stung his
nose so that he awoke. As soon as the hare was
awake, he roused the fox, and the fox roused the
wolf, and the wolf roused the bear, and the bear
roused the lion.

And when the lion awoke and saw that the
maiden was gone, and his master was dead, he
began to roar frightfully and cried, "Who has done
that? Bear, why did you not waken me?"

The bear asked the wolf, "Why did you not
waken me?" and the wolf the fox, "Why did you not
waken me?" and the fox the hare, "Why did you not
waken me?"

The poor hare alone did not know what answer
to make, and the blame rested with him.

Then they were just going to fall upon him, but he entreated them and said, "Kill me not, I will bring our master to life again. I know a mountain on which a root grows which, when placed in the mouth of any one, cures him of all illness and every wound. But the mountain lays two hundred hours journey from here."

The lion said, "In four-and-twenty hours must you have run thither and have come back, and have brought the root with you."

Then the hare sprang away, and in four-and-twenty hours he was back, and brought the root with him.

The lion put Baldwyn's head on again, and the hare placed the root in his mouth, and immediately everything united together again, and Baldwyn's heart beat and life came back.

The Turn Around[40]

Then the huntsman awoke, and was alarmed when he did not see the maiden, and thought, "She must have gone away whilst I was sleeping, in order to get rid of me."

The lion in his great haste had put his master's head on the wrong way round, but Baldwyn did not observe it because of his melancholy thoughts about the King's daughter. But at noon, when he was going to eat something, he saw that his head was turned backwards and could not understand it, and asked the animals what had happened to him in his sleep.

Then the lion told him that they, too, had all fallen asleep from weariness, and on awaking, had found him dead with his head cut off, that the hare had brought the life-giving root, and that he, in his haste, had laid hold of the head the wrong way, but that he would repair his mistake.

Then he tore Baldwyn's head off again, turned it round, and the hare healed it with the root.

The huntsman, however, was still sad at heart, and remained in a gloomy mood. Baldwyn soon travelled about the world, and made his animals dance before people.

Ye Tale Well Worn

To The Lodge[41]

Meanwhile, the three apprentices went to the village lodge, and the lodge-keeper came to meet them, and asked if they wished for anything to eat?

The first replied, "All three of us."

"Yes," said the host, "that is what I mean."

The second said, "For money."

"Of course," said the host.

The third said, "And quite right too!"

"Certainly it is right," said the host.

Good meat and drink were now brought to them, and they were well waited on.

After the dinner came the payment, and the lodge-keeper gave the bill to the one who said, "All three of us," the second said, "For money," and the third, "and quite right too!"

"Indeed it is right," said the host, "all three pay, and without money I can give nothing."

They, however, paid still more than he had asked. The lodgers, who were looking on, said, "These people must be mad."

"Yes, indeed they are," said the host, "they are not very wise."

So they stayed some time in the lodge, and said nothing else but, "All three of us", "For money", and "And quite right too!" But they saw and knew all that was going on.

It so happened that a great merchant came with a large sum of money, and said, "Sir host, take care of my money for me, here are three crazy apprentices who might steal it from me."

The host did as he was asked. As he was carrying the trunk into his room, he felt that it was heavy with gold. Thereupon he gave the three apprentices a lodging below, but the merchant came up-stairs into a separate apartment.

When it was midnight, and the host thought that all were asleep, he came with his wife, and they had an axe and struck the rich merchant dead; and after they had murdered him they went to bed again.

When it was day there was a great outcry; the merchant lay dead in bed bathed in blood. All the guests ran at once but the host said, "The three crazy apprentices have done this;" the lodgers confirmed it, and said, "It can have been no one else."

The lodge-keeper, however, had them called, and said to them, "Have you killed the merchant?"

"All three of us," said the first, "For money," said the second; and the third added, "And quite right too!"

"There now, you hear," said the host, "they confess it themselves."

They were taken to prison, therefore, and were
to be tried. When they saw that things were going
so seriously, they were after all afraid, but at night
the richly-dressed man came and said, "Bear it just
one day longer, and do not play away your luck,
not one hair of your head shall be hurt."

A Morning Break[42]

The next morning the three apprentices were
led to the bar, and the judge said, "Are you the
murderers?"

"All three of us."

"Why did you kill the merchant?"

"For money."

"You wicked wretches, you have no horror of
your sins?"

"And quite right too!"

"They have confessed, and are still stubborn,"
said the judge, "lead them to death instantly."

So they were taken out, and the host had to go
with them into the circle. When they were taken
hold of by the executioner's men, and were just
going to be led up to the scaffold where the
headsman was standing with naked sword, a coach
drawn by four blood-red chestnut horses came up
suddenly, driving so fast that fire flashed from the
stones, and someone made signs from the window
with a white handkerchief.

Then said the headsman, "It is a pardon
coming," and "Pardon! pardon!" was called from
the carriage also. Then a man stepped out as a very
noble gentleman, beautifully dressed, and said,

"You three are innocent; you may now speak, make known what you have seen and heard."

Then said the eldest, "We did not kill the merchant, the murderer is standing there in the circle," and he pointed to the lodge-keeper. "In proof of this, go into his cellar, where many others whom he has killed are still hanging."

Then the judge sent the executioner's men thither, and they found it was as the apprentices said, and when they had informed the judge of this, he caused the lodge-keeper to be led up, and his head was cut off.

Then said the man to the three, "Now I have got the soul which I wanted to have, and you are free, and have money for the rest of your lives."

The Return[43]

As fate would have it, Helmer traveled far and wide and soon returned to the town from which he came.

He went to the best inn, ordered himself handsome clothes, and then bade the landlord furnish him a room as handsome as possible. When it was ready and he had taken possession of it, Helmer summoned the manikin and said: "I have served the tyrant faithfully, but he has dismissed me, and left me to hunger, and now I want to take my revenge."

"What am I to do?" asked the little man.

"Late at night, when the Tyrant's daughter is to bed, bring her here in her sleep, she shall pay for her father's ills and do servant's work for me."

The manikin said: "That is an easy thing for me to do, but a very dangerous thing for you, for if it is discovered, you shall fare ill."

When low twelve had struck, the door sprang open, and the gnome carried in the princess.

"Aha! are you there?" cried the mercenary, "get to your work at once! Fetch the broom and sweep the chamber."

When she had done this, Helmer ordered her to come to his chair, and then he stretched out his feet and said: "Pull off my boots," and then he threw them in her face, and made her pick them up again, and clean and brighten them. She, however, did everything he bade her, without opposition, silently and with half-shut eyes. When the first cock crowed, the manikin carried her back to the royal palace, and laid her in her bed.

Next morning when the returned princess arose she went to her father, and told him that she had had a very strange dream. "I was carried through the streets with the rapidity of lightning," said she, "and taken into a mercenary's room, and I had to wait upon him like a servant, sweep his room, clean his boots, and do all kinds of menial work. It was only a dream, and yet I am just as tired as if I really had done everything."

"The dream may have been true," said the tyrant. "I will give you a piece of advice. Fill your pocket full of peas, and make a small hole in the pocket, and then if you are carried away again, they will fall out and leave a track in the streets."

But unseen by the tyrant, the manikin was standing beside him when he said that, and heard all. At night when the sleeping princess was again carried through the streets, some peas certainly did fall out of her pocket, but they made no track, for the crafty manikin had just before scattered peas in every street there was. And again the princess was compelled to do servant's work until cock-crow.

Next morning the tyrant sent his people out to seek the track, but it was all in vain, for in every street poor children were sitting, picking up peas, and saying: "It must have rained peas last night."

"We must think of something else," said the tyrant; "keep your shoes on when you go to bed, and before you come back from the place where you are taken, hide one of them there, I will soon contrive to find it."

The manikin heard this plot, and at night when the mercenary again ordered him to bring the princess, revealed it to him, and told him that he knew of no expedient to counteract this stratagem and that if the shoe were found in the mercenary's inn room it would go badly with him. "Do what I bid you," replied the mercenary, and again this third night the princess was obliged to work like a servant, but before she went away, she hid her shoe under the bed.

Next morning the tyrant had the entire town searched for his daughter's shoe. It was found in the mercenary's room, and the mercenary himself, who at the entreaty of the gnome had gone outside the gate, was soon brought back, and thrown into prison.

A Royal Mystery[44]

Meanwhile, back in King Ultman's realm, the three princesses, all now well, walked during the day within the palace garden, for the king was a great lover of all kinds of fine trees.

But there was one tree for which he had such affection, that if anyone dared pluck a single apple from it he wished him a thousand fathoms underground.

And it was indeed a beautiful tree. When harvest time came, its apples were all as red as blood and unblemished.

The three princesses went daily beneath this tree, and looked to see if the wind had blown down an apple, but they never by any chance found one. At each harvest, the tree would be found so loaded with them that it was almost at breaking, and the branches hung clear down to the ground.

But even then, look as they may, the three princesses would walk slowly away from it in disappointment. The tree did not give up its fruit readily.

In the evenings, the three slept together in one room, where their beds rested next to one another side by side. And once in bed, when they were lying there ready for sleep, King Ultman would shut their door firmly and bar it rigidly, allowing none to pass or repass[cc].

However, when he opened it each morning he saw with great dismay that each of their shoes had been worn to pieces. No matter who would consider this oddity, no one could determine how it had happened.

With great frustration, the king proclaimed that whomsoever could discover the reason behind the puzzling shoe wear occurring each night could chose one of them for his wife and become ruler of a portion of his realm as well. However, anyone who tried to solve this mystery, and failed to make the discovery after three days and nights, would court the rope-maker's daughter[dd] for failing.

Immediately, a greedy prince presented himself, offering to undertake the venture. He was well received, and that evening was taken to a room adjacent to the bedroom. A bed was made for him there, and he was told to watch where they went and for how the shoes would wear. So they would not be able to do anything in secret, or go out to some other place, the door to their room was left open.

However, the prince's eyes felt as heavy as lead, and he fell asleep. When he awoke the next morning, the three pairs of shoes all had holes in

---

[cc] Repass: pass again, especially on the way back.
[dd] The Rope-maker's Daughter: Hangman's noose

their soles from undue wear. The same thing happened the second and the third evenings, and he was soon hanged for his shortcomings.

Many others came to try this risky venture, but they too failed and were likewise dispatched soon thereafter.

The Soldier[45]

Now it happened too that Ghislain[ee], a poor and recently discharged soldier, who had served well his proper time as such, was making his way home through the city where King Ultman lived. The soldier had enlisted years before, conducted himself bravely, and was always at the very front of the action when harm and havoc were at its worst. As long as the war lasted all went well, but with its end he was dismissed, and his captain said he was free to go wherever he wanted to.

Being long past his youth and not wanting to burden his parents, he had gone to his brothers and asked them to support him until there was another war.

His brothers, however, were hardhearted and told him, "What can we do with you? We have no work for you. See that you go and make a living for yourself. Be gone and fare well"

The discharged soldier, and now rejected brother, had nothing left but his gun and a longing to do battle, so, he put it on his shoulder and he went forth into the world.

[ee] Ghislain: [German origin] means "Oath"

An Encounter[46]

An old woman called, "Gudrun[ff]", met him on the king's road and asked him where he was going. "I'm not exactly sure myself," he said, and then, knowing the news of the king's predicament, jokingly added, "But I would certainly like to discover why those princesses' shoes were worn to pieces, and become king of my own realm."

"Oh, that is not so difficult to find out" quickly replied the old woman. Startled by her statement but knowing the old woman was sincere, Ghislain retorted, "and what must this discharged destitute soldier provide to you in return for your generous thoughts?"

"You shall overhear an old man in need many years from now", she said, "and if I tell you what I know, you shall assure me now that he shall want for nothing after you cross his path."

The poor soldier without hesitation promised he would.

She looked through his eyes and into his heart and said quite firmly, "Very well. Do not drink the wine that these princesses will bring you in the evening."

Then she gave him a cloak and added, "When they think you asleep and go to depart, you should follow the three with them knowing no better. Put this on when you do and you will become invisible to all."

[ff] Gudrun: [German origin] means "She who knows the secrets of battle"

The Pursuit[47]

Having received her good advice from the old woman, the soldier became serious, took heart, went to King Ultman, and announced himself as a suitor.

He, like the others, was well received, and was given royal clothes to wear. That evening at bedtime he was escorted to the anteroom. Just as he was going to bed, Galiana, one of the king's daughters, brought him a goblet of wine. However, he had tied a sponge beneath his chin and let the wine run into it, drinking not a single drop himself.

He lay down, and after a little while began to snore as if he were in the deepest sleep. The three princesses heard him and laughed. The middle one said, "He could have spared his life as well!"

Then they got up, opened their wardrobes, chests, and closets, took out their best clothes, and made themselves beautiful in front of their mirrors, all the time jumping about in anticipation. Only the youngest one said, "I'm not sure. You are all very happy, but I'm afraid that something bad is going to happen!"

"Don't be silly," said Galiana. "You are always so afraid! Have you forgotten how many princes have been here for nothing? I wouldn't even have had to give this soldier a sleeping potion. He would never have awakened."

Under Way[48]

When they were ready, they first approached the soldier, but he did not move at all, and as soon

as they thought it was safe, the oldest one went to her bed and knocked upon it thrice. Upon the third knock, it immediately sank beneath the floor, and they all climbed down through the opening, one after the other, Galiana leading the way. The discharged soldier saw everything, and without hesitating he put on the cloak and followed after the youngest one. Halfway down the stairs he stepped on her dress. Frightened, she called out, "Who's there? Who is holding my dress?"

"Don't be so stupid," said Galiana. "You just caught yourself on a hook."

They continued until they came to a magnificent walkway between rows of trees. Their leaves were all made of silver, and they shone and glistened. The soldier thought to himself, "You'd better take some proof," and he broke off a twig.

A loud cracking sound came from the tree. The youngest one called out again, "It's not right. Didn't you hear that sound?"

Galiana said, "That is just a joyful salute that they are firing because soon we will have disenchanted our princes."

Then they came to a walkway where the trees were all made of gold, and finally to a third one, where they were made of clear diamonds. He broke a twig from each of these. The cracking sound frightened the youngest one each time, but Galiana insisted that it was only the sounds of joyful salutes.

They continued on until they came to a large body of water. Three boats were there, and in each boat there sat a handsome prince waiting for them. Each prince took a princess into his boat.

The soldier sat next to the youngest princess, and her prince said, "I don't know why the boat is so sluggish today. I have to row with all my strength in order to make it go."

"It must be the warm weather," said the youngest princess. "It's too hot for me as well."

On the other side of the water there was a beautiful, brightly illuminated castle. Joyful

music, kettle drums, and trumpets sounded forth.

They rowed over and went inside.

Each prince danced with his princess. The invisible soldier danced along as well, and whenever a princess held up a goblet of wine, he drank it empty as she lifted it to her mouth. This always frightened the youngest one, but Galiana silenced her every time.

They danced there until three o'clock the next morning when their shoes were danced to pieces and they had to stop. The princes rowed them back across the water. This time the soldier took a seat next to the oldest princess in the lead boat. They took leave from their princes on the bank and promised to come back the next night.

When they were on the steps the soldier ran ahead and got into bed. When the three tired princesses came in slowly, he was again snoring so loudly that they all could hear him.

"We are safe from him," they said.

Then they took off their beautiful clothes and put them away, placed their worn out shoes under their beds, and went to bed.

On The Third Day[49]

The next morning the soldier said nothing, for he wanted to see the amazing event once again. He went along the second night and also the third, and everything happened just as before. Each time they danced until their shoes were in pieces. The third time he also took away a goblet as a piece of evidence.

The hour came when he was to give his answer, and he brought the three twigs and the goblet before King Ultman. The three princesses stood behind the door and listened to what he had to say.

The king asked, "What is the cause of their shoes being worn to pieces?"

He answered, "Your three daughters wore them to pieces dancing in an underground castle with three enchanted princes."

Then he told the whole story and brought forth the pieces of evidence he had secured each night.

The king was astonished, summoned his daughters and asked them if the soldier had told the truth.

Seeing that their activities had been revealed, and that their denials would do no good, they admitted to everything.

Then King Ultman asked him which one he wanted for a wife. He answered, "I myself am no longer young, so if the oldest one would have me, I shall willingly wed."

The eldest princess gladly agreed and their wedding was to be held soon thereafter, with a portion of the realm to be his following the king's demise.

The Garden[50]

Much relieved that their father was so lenient of their nightly activities, the three princesses took to their daily garden walk. And it was on that day that King Ultman's youngest daughter had a great desire for an apple, and said to her sisters, "Our father loves us far too much to wish us underground, it is my belief that he would only do that to people who were strangers."

And while she was speaking, the young princess plucked off quite a large apple, and ran to her sisters, saying, "Just taste, my dear sisters, for never in my life have I tasted anything so delightful."

Then the two others also ate some of the apple, whereupon all three sank deep down into the earth, where they could hear no cock crow.

When high noon came, the king wished to call them to come to dinner, but they were nowhere to be found. He sought them everywhere in the palace and garden, but could not find them.

Then he was much troubled, and made known to the whole land that whosoever brought his daughters back again should have one of them to wife and a portion of the realm upon his death.

When hearing this, the discharged soldier, having been already promised this very thing with nothing now to show for his efforts, felt deceived, bid the king farewell and went wandering off into

the forest, dejected and no longer knowing what to do with himself.

A Hunting Party[51]

Meanwhile, the young men of the realm went about the country in search for the three princesses. As locusts, there was no counting them, for every one of them had heard of King Ultman's promise and wanted for himself the rewards.

Three young huntsmen also went out in search. When they had travelled about for seven days, they arrived at a great castle, in which were beautiful apartments. In one room a table was laid on which were delicate dishes which were still so warm that they were steaming. But in the whole of the castle a human being was neither to be seen nor heard.

They waited there for half a day, and the food still remained warm and smoking, and at length they were so hungry that they sat down and ate.

Well fed, they soon agreed with each other that they would stay and live in that castle, and that one of them, who should be chosen by casting lots, should remain there, while the two others sought the king's daughters.

The Sticky Mess[52]

They cast lots, and the lot fell on the eldest; so next day the two younger went out to seek, and the eldest had to stay home.

At high noon came a small manikin and begged for a piece of bread. Then the huntsman took the bread which he had found there, and cut a round off the loaf. He was about to give it to him, but whilst he was giving it to the manikin, the latter let it fall, and asked the eldest huntsman to be so good as to give him that piece again.

The huntsman was about to do so and stooped, on which the little manikin took a stick, seized him by the hair, and gave him a good beating.

Next day, the middle huntsman stayed at home, and he fared no better. When the two others returned in the evening, the eldest said, "Well, how have you got on?"

"Oh, very badly," said he, and then they lamented their misfortune together, but they said nothing about it to Hewitt[gg], the youngest, for they did not like him at all, and always called him "Stupid", because he did not exactly belong to the forest.

On the third day the youngest stayed at home, and again the small manikin came and begged for a piece of bread. When the youth gave it to him, the small visitor let it fall as he did before, and asked the young huntsman to be so good as to give him that piece again.

Then said Hewitt to the little manikin, "What!

Can't you pick up that piece yourself? If you won't take as much trouble as that for your daily bread, you don't deserve to have it."

Then the manikin grew very angry and said the huntsman was to do it, but Hewitt would not, and took the manikin, and gave him a

---

[gg] Hewitt: [German origin] means "smart little one"

thorough beating.

Then the manikin screamed terribly, and cried, "Stop, stop, and let me go, and I will tell you where King Ultman's daughters are."

When Hewitt heard that, he left off beating him and the manikin told him that he was a gnome[hh], and that there were more than a thousand like him, and that if he would go with him he would show him where the king's daughters were.

Then he revealed to him a deep well, but there was no water in it. And the gnome said that he knew well that the companions the young huntsman had with him did not intend to deal honorably with him. Therefore if he wished to deliver the king's daughters, he must do it alone.

The gnome continued and said that the two older brothers would also be very glad to recover the king's daughters for themselves, but would not want to have any trouble or danger in doing so.

Hewitt was to therefore take a large basket, and he must seat himself in it with his hanger[ii] and a bell, and be let down. Below were to be found three rooms, and in each of them was a princess, with a many-headed dragon, whose heads she was to comb and trim, but he must cut them off. And having shared all this, the gnome vanished.

[hh] Gnome: a legendary dwarfish creature supposed to guard the earth's treasures underground.

[ii] Hanger: A short sword that may be hung from a belt.

Ye Going Down

A Deal[53]

Meanwhile, the much disappointed Ghislain now wandered the wilderness with no gain for his efforts and knowing not what to do with himself.

The soldier soon came to a large heath, on which nothing was to be seen but a circle of trees. Filled with sorrow, he sat down beneath them to perpend his fate.

"I have no money," he thought, "and am no better off than when I set out. The only trade I have ever learned is that of making war, and since they have made peace, they can no longer use me, so I see that I shall soon starve."

Suddenly he heard a rustling sound, and when he looked around, a strange little man was standing before him.

"What's the matter?" the little man said to him. "You look so gloomy."

"I'm hungry, depressed and have no money," said the soldier.

"I know what you are in need of," said the man. "You shall have money and property, as much as you, with all your might, can squander away. But I must know if you are worthy, fearless and committed, so that I won't be wasting my efforts for nothing."

"A soldier and fear -- how can those go together?" he answered, "You can put me to the test." He then insisted, *"Try me!"*

"Oh, you boast very well," answered the little man, "Let me see your word's worth. Have a look behind you."

The soldier turned around and saw a large growling bear with green fur running towards him.

"Aha," shouted the soldier, "I'll tickle your nose until you lose your desire for growling."

Then taking aim at the bear, he shot it in the snout, and it fell down motionless.

"I see quite well," said the little man, "that you do not lack for courage, but your commitment requires something more. There is one more condition that you will have to fulfill should you want for not."

"If it does not endanger my soul," answered the soldier, who knew quite well who was standing before him. "Otherwise I'll have nothing to do with it."

"You'll see about that for yourself," answered the little man. "If you hire yourself out to me and will be my servant," the little man said, "you'll have enough for the rest of your life. But you've got to serve me seven years, and after that you'll be free. And to further test your resolve, there's just one other thing I've got to tell you about this obligation: during your time in my employment, you're not allowed to wash yourself, comb your hair, trim your beard, cut your nails or hair, or wipe your eyes or nose, or pray outwardly. Furthermore, should you die during these seven years, you are mine. However, should you stay alive, you are free and rich as well, for all the rest of your life."

The soldier thought about his desperate situation, and having faced death so often before, he decided to risk it now as well, and he entered into the agreement.

"If that's the way it must be, let's get on with it," the soldier said.

"Good" the little man exclaimed and with agreement reached, he pulled the green fur off the bear and said, "This shall be your cloak, and your bed as well, for you are to sleep on it, and you are not allowed to lie in any other bed."

Ghislain went away with the little man, who led him straight to hell and told him what his chores were: he was to tend the fires under the kettles in which the damned souls were sitting, sweep the house clean and carry the dirt out the door, and keep everything in order.

However, he was told never to peek into the kettles, or things would go badly for him.

"I understand," said the soldier. "I'll take good care of everything.

So the little man set out again on his travels, and the soldier began his duty. He put fuel on the fires, swept and carried the dirt out the door, and did everything just as he was ordered.

When the old devil returned, he checked to see if everything had been done according to his instructions, nodded his approval, and went off again.

The Well[54]

Meanwhile, it was late in the evening when the two huntsmen came back to the castle. They quickly asked how their little brother had got on.

Hewitt said, "pretty well so far," and that he had seen no one except at high noon when a little manikin had come begging for a piece of bread. He said that he had given some to him, but that the manikin had let it fall. The little man had asked him to pick it up again; but as he did not choose to do that, the manikin had begun to lose his temper because he had done what the manikin said he ought not. Hewitt said that he had given the short fellow a beating, on which the manikin quickly told him where the king's daughters were.

Then the two were so angry at this that they grew green and yellow, but they held their tongues.

The next morning all three went to the well together, and drew lots to see who should first seat himself in the basket, and again the lot fell on the eldest, and he was to seat himself in it, and take the bell with him.

Then he said, "If I ring, you must draw me up again immediately."

When he had gone down for a short distance, he rang, and they at once drew him up again.

Then the second seated himself in the basket, but he did just the same as the first.

Then it was the turn of the youngest, but he let himself be lowered quite to the bottom.

When Hewitt had got out of the basket, he took his hanger, and went and stood outside the first door and listened, and heard the dragon snoring quite loudly. He opened the door slowly, and one of the princesses was sitting there, and had three red dragon's heads lying upon her lap, and was combing them.

Then Hewitt took his hanger and hewed at them hard, and the three fell off. The princess sprang up, threw her arms round his neck, embraced and kissed him repeatedly, and took her stomacher[jj], which was made of red rubied silver,

---

[jj] Stomacher: a) A heavily embroidered or jeweled garment formerly worn over the chest and stomach, especially by women.

and hung it round his neck[kk].

Then Hewitt took hold once again of his hanger, and went and stood outside the second door and listened. He heard a second dragon snoring quite loudly. He opened the door slowly, and another of the princesses was sitting there, and had five white dragon's heads lying upon her lap, and was combing them.

Then Hewitt took his hanger and hewed at them hard, and the five fell off. The princess sprang up, threw her arms round his neck, embraced and kissed him repeatedly, and took her stomacher, which was made of pure white gold, and hung it round his neck.

The he took hold once again of his hanger, and went and stood outside the third door and listened. He heard a third dragon snoring quite loudly. He opened the door slowly, and the last of the princesses was sitting there, and had seven black dragon's heads lying upon her lap, and was combing them.

Then Hewitt took his hanger and hewed at them hard, and the seven fell off. The princess sprang up, threw her arms round his neck, embraced and kissed him repeatedly, and took her

---

b) (obsolete) [15th-8th c.] A type of men's waistcoat.

c) (now chiefly historical) An ornamental cloth, often embellished with embroidery or jewelry, worn by women under the lacing of a bodice.

[kk] Therefore covering his chest and stomach.

stomacher, which was made of pure clear
diamonds, and hung it round his neck.

And as they were now reunited, they all
rejoiced, and embraced him and kissed him
without stopping.

With the princesses found and the dragons
dispatched, Hewitt approached the well bottom
and rang his bell very loud, so that those above
heard him. He placed the princesses one after the
other in the basket, and had them all drawn up.

But when it came his own turn, he remembered
the words of the gnome, who had warned him that
his brothers did not mean well by him.

So Hewitt took a great ashlar[ll] which was lying
there at well's bottom, and placed it within the
basket and signaled his brothers above. When it
was raised about half way up the well his false
brothers above cut the rope. The basket, with the
rough ashlar, crashed to the ground below.

Thinking now that Hewitt was surely dead, they
ran away with the three princesses, forcing them to
promise to tell their father that it was they who had
delivered them. They then went to King Ultman,
and each demanded for themselves a princess in
marriage.

Gnomes[55]

In the underground, the youngest huntsman
wandered about the three chambers in great
trouble, fully expecting to have to end his days
down there. As he traveled, he saw, hanging on the

[ll] Hewn stone

wall, a bone flute. He said to it quite indignantly, "Why do you hang there taunting me, no one can be merry down here?"

Hewitt looked at the dragons' heads likewise and said, "You too cannot help me now."

He walked backwards and forwards for such a long time that he made the surface of the stone ground below quite smooth.

But at last other thoughts came to his mind, for he had nothing down there to distract him and he took the flute from the wall, and played a few notes through it.

To Hewitt's surprise, with each note he played suddenly appeared a number of gnomes, and with every note he sounded thereafter others came forth.

Delighted, he continued to play to his heart's content and the three chambers were soon entirely filled with gnomes.

But, Hewitt soon tired and pulled the whistle from his lips. As he did, they asked, in one unified voice, what he desired most.

He took no time at all to say, "I wish to get above ground and back to the light of day."

Upon Hewitt's request, they seized him by every hair that grew from his head, and thus they flew with him on to the earth above.

When he was again above ground, he at once went to King Ultman's palace. Perchance he arrived just as the wedding of one princess was about to take place, and he went to the room where the king and his three daughters were.

When the three saw Hewitt they fainted. Hereupon the king was angry, and ordered him to be put in prison at once, because he thought the young huntsman must have done some injury to them.

However, when the princesses came to themselves, they entreated the king to set Hewitt free again. The king asked them why, and they said that they could not tell him.

But their father, knowing the importance of keeping true to one's word, said that they were to tell the truth to the stove. And with that said, he went out, listened at the door, and heard everything.

Upon hearing the details of their rescue and the huntsman's deliberate actions against their brother, he caused the two false brothers to be thrown into the well for their mistreatments and deceit. However, to Hewitt, he gave his youngest daughter and willed to him a portion of his realm upon his death.

The Fires[56]

Back in hell, every moment the discharged soldier spent stoking the fires, his appearance slowly transformed.

At first, his appearance was still acceptable, but as his time in hell took its toll, Ghislain soon looked like a monster. His hair covered nearly his entire face. His beard looked like a piece of coarse felt cloth. His fingers had claws, and his face was so covered with dirt that if someone had planted cress[mm] on it, it would have grown.

And for the first time, with nothing of appearance to distract him, the soldier took a good look around hell.

There were dark kettles all about it, and they were boiling and bubbling with tremendous fires under each one of them. Ghislain would have given his life to know what was in them if the little man had not strictly forbidden it.

Finally, he could no longer restrain himself. The soldier lifted the lid of the first kettle a little and looked inside, only to see his intemperate sergeant sitting there.

"Aha, you crumb!" Ghislain said with scorn. "Fancy meeting *you* here! You used to step on me, but now I've got you under *my* foot."

He let the lid drop quickly, stirred the fire underneath, and added fresh dry wood until it glowed red hot.

This kept him very happy, for a while. Ghislain kept the fire burning hotter under that kettle than all the rest.

After a while, his curiosity got the better of him once again and he moved to the second kettle, lifted the lid a little, and peeked inside. There sat his weak lieutenant.

[mm] Cress: a plant of the cabbage family, typically having small white flowers and pungent leaves. Some kinds are edible and are eaten raw as salad.

"Aha, you crumb!" Ghislain said with more scorn. "Fancy meeting *you* here! You used to step on me, but now I've got you under *my* foot."

He shut the lid down tight and added logs to the fire until it flared white hot under the kettle.

This kept him very pleased, for a while. Ghislain kept the fire burning even hotter under that kettle than all the rest.

Eventually he wanted to see who was sitting in the third kettle. Soon, the soldier moved to the third kettle, lifted the lid wide, and peered inside, and it turned out to be his imprudent general.

"Aha, you crumb!" Ghislain said with further scorn. "Fancy meeting *you* here! You used to step on me, but now I've got you under *my* foot."

This time he added more logs, got out a bellows and pumped it vigorously until the hell fire blazed blue under it.

And so it was that Ghislain served out his seven years in hell. He never washed, combed himself, trimmed his beard, cut his nails, or wiped his eyes or nose or prayed outwardly.

And the fires were never hotter.

Ye Dinner Guests

Homecoming[57]

It came to pass that precisely at the end of one year Baldwyn came back to the same town where he had delivered King Wilford's virgin daughter, Tugenda, from the dragon, and this time the town was gaily hung with red cloth.

Then he said to the innkeeper, "What does this mean? Last year the town was all hung with black crape, what means the red cloth this day?"

The host answered, "Last year our King's virgin daughter was to have been delivered over to the dragon. But the marshal fought with it and killed it, and so on the morrow their wedding is to be solemnized. That is why the town was then hung with black crape for mourning, and is today covered with red cloth for joy."

Next day when the wedding was to take place, the huntsman said at high noon to the host, "Do you believe, sir host that while I'm with you here today, I shall eat bread from the King's own table?"

"Nay," said the host, "I would bet a hundred pieces of gold that that will not come true."

A Wager Taken[58]

Baldwyn accepted the wager, and set against it a purse with just the same number of gold pieces.

Then he called the hare and said, "Go, my dear runner, and fetch me some of the bread which the King is eating."

Now the little hare was the lowest of the animals, and could not transfer this order to any the others, but had to get on his legs himself.

"Alas!" thought he, "if I bound through the streets thus alone, the butchers' dogs will all be after me."

It happened as he expected, and the dogs came after him and wanted to make holes in his good skin. But he sprang away, as fast as one could see one running and sheltered himself in a sentry-box without the guard being aware of it.

Then the dogs came and wanted to have him out, but the soldier did not understand a jest, and struck them with the butt-end of his gun, till they ran away yelling and howling.

As soon as the hare saw that the way was clear, he ran into the palace and straight to the King's daughter, sat down under her chair, and scratched at her foot.

The Daily Bread[59]

Then Tugenda said, "Will you get away?" thinking it was her dog.

The hare scratched her foot for the second time, and she again said, "Will you get away?" still thinking it was her dog.

But the hare did not let itself be turned from its purpose, and scratched her for the third time.

Then she peeped down, and knew the hare by its collar.

Tugenda took him on her lap, carried him into her chamber, and said, "Dear Hare, what do you want?"

He answered, "My master, who killed the dragon, is here, and has sent me to ask for a loaf of bread like that which the King eats."

Then she was full of joy and had the baker summoned, and ordered him to bring a loaf such as was eaten by the King.

The little hare said, "But the baker must

likewise carry it thither for me, that the butchers' dogs may do no harm to me."

The baker carried it for him as far as the door of the inn, and then the hare got on his hind legs, took the loaf in his front paws, and carried it to his master.

Then said Baldwyn, "Behold, sir host, the hundred pieces of gold are mine."

A Meaty Need[60]

The host was astonished, but the huntsman went on to say, "Yes, sir host, I have the bread, but now I will likewise have some of the King's roast meat."

The host said, "I should indeed like to see that," but he would make no more wagers.

Baldwyn called the fox and said, "My little fox, go and fetch me some roast meat, such as the King eats."

The red fox knew the bye-ways better, and went by holes and corners without any dog seeing him, seated himself under the chair of the King's daughter, and scratched her foot.

Then Tugenda looked down and recognized the fox by its collar, took him into her chamber with her and said, "Dear Fox, what do you want?"

He answered, "My master, who killed the dragon, is here, and has sent me. I am to ask for some roast meat such as the King is eating."

Then she made the cook come, who was obliged to prepare a roast joint, the same as was eaten by the King, and to carry it for the fox as far as the door.

Then the fox took the dish, waved away with his tail the flies which had settled on the meat, and then carried it to his master.

"Behold, sir host," said Baldwyn, "bread and meat are here but now I will also have proper vegetables with it, such as are eaten by the King."

Fiber Filling[61]

Then Baldwyn called the wolf, and said, "Dear Wolf, go thither and fetch me vegetables such as the King eats."

Then the wolf went straight to the palace, as he feared no one, and when he got to the King's daughter's chamber, he twitched at the back of her dress, so that she was forced to look round. She recognized him by his collar, and took him into her chamber with her, and said, "Dear Wolf, what do you want?"

He answered, "My master, who killed the dragon, is here, I am to ask for some vegetables, such as the King eats."

Then Tugenda made the cook come, and he had to make ready a dish of vegetables, such as the King ate, and had to carry it for the wolf as far as the door, and then the wolf took the dish from him, and carried it to his master.

"Behold, sir host," said the huntsman, "now I have bread and meat and vegetables, but I will also have some pastry to eat like that which the King eats."

A Sweet Need[62]

He called the bear, and said, "Dear Bear, you are fond of licking anything sweet; go and bring me some confectionery, such as the King eats."

Then the bear trotted to the palace, and everyone got out of his way, but when he went to the guard, they presented their muskets, and would not let him go into the royal palace. But he got up on his hind legs, and gave them a few boxes on the ears, right and left, with his paws, so that the whole watch broke up, and then he went straight to the King's daughter, placed himself behind her, and growled a little.

Then Tugenda looked behind her, knew the bear, and bade him go into her room with her, and said, "Dear Bear, what do you want?"

He answered, "My master, who killed the dragon, is here, and I am to ask for some confectionery, such as the King eats."

Then she summoned her confectioner, who had to bake confectionery such as the King ate, and carry it to the door for the bear; then the bear first licked up the comfits[nn] which had rolled down, and then he stood upright, took the dish, and carried it to his master.

"Behold, sir host," said Baldwyn, "now I have bread, meat, vegetables and confectionery, but I will drink wine also, and such as the King drinks."

The Good Spirits[63]

Baldwyn called his lion to him and said, "Dear Lion, you yourself like to drink till you are intoxicated, go and fetch me some wine, such as is drunk by the King."

Then the lion strode through the streets, and the people fled from him, and when he came to the watch, they wanted to bar the way against him, but he did but roar once, and they all ran away.

Then the lion went to the royal apartment, and knocked at the door with his tail. Then the King's daughter came forth, and was almost afraid of the lion, but Tugenda knew him by the golden clasp of her necklace, and bade him go with her into her

---

[nn] candies consisting of a nut, seed, or other center coated in sugar.

chamber, and said, "Dear Lion, what will you have?"

He answered, "My master, who killed the dragon, is here, and I am to ask for some wine such as is drunk by the King."

Then she bade the cup-bearer be called, who was to give the lion some wine like that which was drunk by the King. The lion said, "I will go with him, and see that I get the right wine."

Then he went down with the cup-bearer, and when they were below, the cup-bearer wanted to draw him some of the common wine that was drunk by the King's servants, but the lion said, "Stop, I will taste the wine first," and he drew half a measure, and swallowed it down at one draught.

"No," said he, "that is not right."

The cup-bearer looked at him askance, but went on, and was about to give him some out of another barrel which was for the King's marshal.

The lion said, "Stop, let me taste the wine first," and drew half a measure and drank it. "That is better, but still not right," said he.

Then the cup-bearer grew angry and said, "How can a stupid animal like you understand wine?"

But the lion gave him a blow behind the ears, which made him fall down by no means gently, and when he had got up again, he conducted the lion quite silently into a little cellar apart, where the King's wine lay, from which no one ever drank.

The lion first drew half a measure and tried the wine, and then he said, "That may possibly be the right sort", and bade the cup-bearer fill six bottles of it.

And now they went upstairs again, but when the lion came out of the cellar into the open air, he reeled here and there, and was rather drunk, and the cup-bearer was forced to carry the wine as far as the door for him, and then the lion took the handle of the basket in his mouth, and took it to his master.

Baldwyn said, "Behold, sir host, here have I bread, meat, vegetables, confectionery and wine such as the King has, and now I will dine with my animals," and he sat down and ate and drank, and gave the hare, the fox, the wolf, the bear, and the lion also to eat and to drink, and was joyful, for he saw that the King's daughter still loved him.

A Royal Invite[64]

And when he had finished his dinner, Baldwyn said, "Sir host, now have I eaten and drunk, as the King eats and drinks, and now I will go to the King's court and marry the King's daughter."

Said the host, "How can that be, when she already has a betrothed husband, and when the wedding is to be solemnized this day?"

Then the huntsman drew forth the handkerchief which the King's daughter had given him on the dragon's hill, and in which were folded the monster's seven tongues, and said, "That which I hold in my hand shall help me to do it."

Then the innkeeper host looked at the handkerchief, and said, "Whatever I believe, I do not believe that, and I am willing to stake my house and courtyard on it."

With that said, Baldwyn, took a bag with a thousand gold pieces, put it on the table, and said, "I stake that on it."

The Rejection[65]

In the meantime, Brother Lustig continued traveling upon his broad and pleasant road, and at length came to a great black door, which was the door of hell.

The journeyman knocked once, and Ghislain stoking the fires behind hell's door ignored it.

The journeyman knocked twice, and the soldier ignored it more.

But Brother Lustig knocked thrice, and at that the soldier stoking the fires could not ignore it further and put down his poker and bellows and came up to the door.

Assuring the door was tightly locked, Ghislain asked, "Who comes here and dares interrupt my great and important work?"

The journeyman replied, "A poor old journeyman who is tired of wandering this world, and wants now to rest his weary bones and

104

cares no longer where that be."

Ghislain cared not for this journeyman's plight. He had his own burdens to tend and went back to his tasking.

In The Shadows[66]

Meanwhile, off in a near recess of hell was the shadow who had limped back to hell. Having overheard the familiar voices at hell's door, he quickly rushed to it and peeped out to confirm who was there.

But when he saw that it was indeed the knapsack carrying journeyman, he was terrified, for this was the very same lone shadow who had been shut up therein with six others, and gaveled within a inch of his life, only to escape to hell from it.

So the shadow pushed the lock-bolt in as firmly and as quickly as he could, ran to his commander, and said, "There is a Fellow outside with a knapsack, who wants to come in, but as you value the lives of all here in hell, don't allow him to enter, or he will wish the whole of hell into his knapsack. He once gave me a frightful gaveling when I was inside it and he divested six others."

So they called out to the journeyman from behind the securely locked door that he was to go away, for he would not get in there!

"If they won't have me here", thought Brother Lustig, "I will see if I can find a place for myself in heaven, for I must be somewhere."

So he turned about and went onwards while the soldier on the other side of the door continued tending his fires, undisturbed.

An Egress[67]

Ghislain's seven years passed so quickly that he was convinced that only six months had gone by.

When the fire stoker's time was completely up, the little man came and said, "Well, my committed friend, what have you been doing all this time?"

"I've tended the fires under these dark kettles, and I've swept and carried the dirt out the door."

"But you also peeked into the dark kettles. Well, you're just lucky that you added more wood to the fire; otherwise, you would have forfeited your life. Now your time is up. Do you want to go back home?"

"Yes," said Ghislain. "I'd like to travel back West to my hometown to see how my father's doing."

"All right, if you want to get your proper reward, you must go and fill your travel-sack with the dirt that you've swept up and this you must take back with you.

Moreover, you must also continue to wear that fur, pray not outwardly, go unwashed, ungroomed and uncombed, with long hair on your head and a long beard, with uncut nails, and with bleary eyes and runny nose.

Furthermore, if anyone asks you whence you come, you must say "From hell." And if anyone asks you who you are, you're to say "I'm the devil's sooty brother and my king as well."

Ye Inn Crowd

The Soldier's Return[68]

Ghislain nodded but said nothing. All that needed to be said was. Indeed, the solder carried out the little man's instructions to the letter, but he was not at all satisfied with the reward.

As soon as he was out in the forest again, he took the travel-sack and wanted to shake it out. But when he opened it, he discovered that his dirt had turned into pure gold.

"Never in my life would I have imagined that," thought the soldier, who was now delighted.

His heart filled with joy, he went into the city.

An innkeeper was standing in front of his inn as the soldier approached. When he caught sight of him, the innkeeper was terrified because the soldier looked so dreadful, even more frightening than a scarecrow.

He called out to him and asked, "Whence come you?"

"From hell" replied the soldier.

"And you are who?" the innkeeper quickly added.

"The devil's sooty brother and my king as well" Ghislain stated boldly.

The innkeeper would not let Ghislain enter though, refusing even to let him have a place in the stable because he was afraid he would frighten the horses.

However, when the soldier reached into his travel-sack and pulled out a handful of gold, the innkeeper's greed softened his resolve and he gave him a room in an outbuilding. He made the journeyman promise though not to let himself be seen, lest the inn should get a bad name.

None the less, the soldier insisted on the finest food service still. He ate and drank his fill but did not wash or comb himself just as the little man had instructed.

Finally, Ghislain lay down to sleep, but could not sleep for he heard a loud moaning in an adjacent room.

His heart kept him from sleep. Restless and concerned, he knocked and opened the door and saw an old man weeping anxiously and flailing his hands above his head.

The soldier went nearer, but the man jumped to his feet and tried to run away.

At last, hearing a human voice coming from the traveler, the man let him approach and talk. With friendly words he succeeded in getting the old man to reveal the cause of his angst.

"I was born a king and have suffered the loss of my three lovely daughters and my integrity" he said. "They were all lost by my selfish wish."

His further folly fouled his fortune when he offered one of his daughters as bride and a portion of his realm to any man who would find them.

"A young huntsman found them" he continued, "but I had lost my wealth since, and now I and my remaining daughters are to starve. I am so poor that the innkeeper shall suffer my fee and I shall surely be sent to prison."

Ghislain was startled. He remembered his promise to the old woman Gudrun years before and saw this as his chance to make good on it.

Moreover, he also recognized the old man to be King Ultman, who once promised his eldest daughter to him should he find out why his daughter's shoes wore out each night.

How neatly things come together he thought.

The Betrothing[69]

No longer disappointed or dejected and now grateful for a chance to honor his obligation, Ghislain said, "Old man, if that is your only problem, I have money enough."

He called for the innkeeper and paid him in full, and then put a bag full of gold into the poor king's pocket.

When the old man saw what the stranger did, and that he was freed from all his debts and troubles, he did not know how to show his gratitude.

"Come with me," he finally said to the soldier. "My youngest has wed, but my two remaining daughters are both miracles of beauty. Choose one of them for your wife. When she hears what you have done for me she will not refuse you. You do look a little strange, to be sure, but she will put you in order again."

This pleased Ghislain well, and the soldier agreed to go with the old man.

When Galiana, the younger of the two, saw him she was so horrified at his face that she screamed. She remained still though and soon looked at him from head to foot. Galiana soon said, "How can I accept a husband who no longer has a human form? The shaved bear that once was here and passed itself off for a man pleased me far better. At least it was wearing a hussar's ⁰⁰ fur and white gloves. If ugliness were his only flaw, I could get used to him. As he is, I shall have nothing to do with him."

The older one, however, said, "Father, dear, he must be a good man to have helped you out of your troubles. If you promised him a bride for doing so,

---

⁰⁰ Hussar: a light horseman.

your word must be kept, as I can no longer be held betrothed to the soldier who abandoned me deep within the earth. If he shall have me, I shall wed him."

It was a pity that the soldier's face was covered with dirt and hair, for otherwise they would have seen how his heart leaped with joy when he heard these words.

Ghislain recognized her to be the eldest princess promised him so many years before. He felt ashamed for his actions but knew he had struggled with far worse fates in his past.

Having paid his debt though, he took a ring from his finger, broke it in two, and gave her one half. He kept the other half himself. He then asked her to take good care of her piece.

A Cleanup Effort[70]

Then Ghislain took his leave of them saying, "I have some unfinished business to which I must immediately attend. If I do not return in forty days you are free, for I shall be dead. So pray God to preserve my life and I shall return."

The poor bride-to-be dressed herself entirely in black, and when she thought about her future bridegroom, tears came into her eyes. From her younger sister she received nothing but contempt and scorn.

"Be careful," said Galiana. "If you do give him your hand, he will hit you with his claws. And beware," she continued with uncaring disdain. "Bears like sweet things, and if he takes a liking to you, he will eat you up."

The bride-to-be said nothing and did not let her sister provoke her.

Ghislain, however, traveled back to the inn, not knowing what to do about his bearlike appearance. The innkeeper welcomed him back this time, fully aware of the riches he could afford and went and unlatched the door himself.

Then the soldier ordered the best room and insisted on the finest service once again. He ate and drank his fill but still did not wash or comb himself as the little man had instructed.

Finally, he lay down to sleep, but the innkeeper could not get the travel-sack of gold out of his mind. Just the thought of it left him no peace. So he crept into the room during the night and stole it.

When the soldier got up the next morning and went to pay the innkeeper, his travel-sack was gone. However, he wasted no words and thought, "It's not your fault that this happened", and he turned around and there he found himself pulled straight back to hell, where he complained about his misfortune to the little man and asked for help.

"You need not my help" he retorted.

And the soldier thought again.

"You're right", Ghislain finally replied. "Come here!" he demanded the little man. "I shall sit down and you will wash and comb me, trim my beard, cut my hair and nails, wash out my eyes and wipe my nose and listen to my prayers."

With this, the little man went to work and the sooty brother soon looked once again the brave soldier and was much better looking than he had ever been before.

When he was finished, the soldier demanded the little man once again. "Take back this cloak and get me another travel-sack full of dirt."

The little man did his bidding, removed the soldiers green fur and handed him a filled travel-sack and said, "Good! Now, go back and tell the innkeeper to give you back your other gold; otherwise, I'll come and fetch him, and he'll have to tend the fires in your place."

The soldier smiled feeling the familiar tug of the travel-sack's weight. He went back up and said to the innkeeper, "You stole my money, and if you don't give it back, you'll go to hell in my place and you'll look just as awful as I did."

The rattled innkeeper gave him back the money and even more besides.

Then he begged the soldier to be quiet about what had happened for an innkeeper known for theft would be soon short of customers.

The Restoration[71]

With his fortune restored and more, Ghislain was quite lighthearted. He went into the town, purchased a splendid velvet jacket, seated himself in a carriage drawn by four white horses, and drove to his betroth's house.

No one recognized him. King Ultman took him for a distinguished colonel and led him into the room where his daughters were sitting. The soldier was given a seat next to Galiana and she soon poured him wine, served him the finest things to eat, and thought that she had never seen a more handsome man in all the world.

The bride-to-be, however, sat across from him in her black dress without raising her eyes or speaking a word.

Finally the soldier asked the father if he would give him one of his daughters for a wife, whereupon Galiana quickly jumped up and ran into her bedroom to put on a splendid dress, for she thought that she was the chosen one.

As soon as he was alone with his bride-to-be, Ghislain brought out his half of the ring and dropped it into a glass of wine, which he handed across the table to her. She took the wine, but when she had drunk it and found the half ring lying at the bottom, her heart began to beat with excitement. She took the other half, which she wore on a ribbon around her neck, put them together, and saw that the two pieces matched perfectly.

Then he said, "Yes. I am your betrothed bridegroom, whom you saw as the unkempt generous stranger. Through God's grace I have regained my humanity and have become clean again."

He went to her, embraced her, and gave her a kiss.

In the meantime Galiana came back in full dress.

When she saw that the older sister had received the handsome man, and heard that he was once the unkempt stranger, she ran out filled with anger and rage, swearing complete vengeance upon all future suitors.

So King Ultman gave the discharged soldier his eldest daughter, who was willing to marry him out of love for her father. And the devil's sooty brother got the king's daughter, and when the old king would pass on, he would get his promised portion of the King's realm as well.

Ye Gathering

An Invite[72]

Now, back in his kingdom, King Wilford in curiosity asked of his daughter, at the royal table, "What did all the wild animals want, which have been coming to you, and going in and out of my palace?"

Tugenda replied, "I may not tell you, but send and have the master of these animals brought, and you will do well."

The King sent a servant to the inn, and invited the stranger, and the servant came just as the twin had laid wager with the innkeeper host.

Then said Baldwyn, "Behold, sir host, now the King sends his servant and invites me, but I do not go in this way."

And he said to the servant, "I request the Lord King to send me royal clothing, and a carriage with seven horses, and servants to attend me."

When the King heard the answer, he said to his daughter, "What shall I do?"

Tugenda said, "Cause him to be fetched as he desires to be, and you will do well."

Then the King sent royal apparel, a carriage with seven horses, and servants to wait on him.

When Baldwyn saw them coming, he said, "Behold, sir host, now I am fetched as I desired to be," and he put on the royal garments, took the handkerchief with the dragon's tongues with him, and drove off to the King.

The Confrontation[73]

When King Wilford saw him coming, he said to his daughter, "How shall I receive him?"

Tugenda answered, "Go to meet him and you will do well."

Then the King went to meet him and led him in, and his animals followed. The King gave him a seat near himself and his daughter, and the marshal, as bridegroom, sat on the other side, who no longer knew the huntsman.

And now at this very moment, the seven heads of the dragon were brought in as a spectacle, and the King said, "The seven heads were cut off the dragon by the marshal, wherefore this day I give him my daughter to wife."

Baldwyn stood up, opened the seven mouths, and said, "Where are the seven tongues of the dragon?"

Then was the marshal terrified, and grew pale and knew not what answer he should make, and at length in his anguish he said, "Dragons have no tongues."

The huntsman said, "Liars ought to have none, but the dragon's tongues are the tokens of the victor," and he unfolded the handkerchief, and there lay all seven inside it.

And he put each tongue in the mouth to which it belonged, and it fitted exactly.

Then he took the handkerchief on which the name of the princess was embroidered, and showed it to the maiden, and asked to whom she had given it, and she replied, "To him who killed the dragon."

And then he called his animals, and took the collar off each of them and the golden clasp from the lion, and showed them to the maiden and asked to whom they belonged.

Tugenda answered, "The necklace and golden clasp were mine, but I divided them among the animals who helped to conquer the dragon."

An Unfolded Tale[74]

Then spake Baldwyn, "When I, tired with the fight, was resting and sleeping, the marshal came and cut off my head. Then he carried away the King's daughter, and gave out that it was he who had killed the dragon. But I proved with the tongues, the handkerchief, and the necklace that he lied."

And then the huntsman related how his animals had healed him by means of a wonderful root, and how he had travelled about with them for one year, and had at length again come there and had learnt the treachery of the marshal by the tavern host's story.

Then the King asked his daughter, "Is it true that this man killed the dragon?"

And Tugenda answered, "Yes, it is true. Now can I reveal the wicked deed of the marshal, as it has come to light without my connivance, for he wrung from me my word to be silent. For this reason, however, did I make the condition that the marriage should not be solemnized for a year and a day."

Then the King bade twelve councilors be summoned who were to pronounce judgment on the marshal, and they sentenced him to be torn in quarters by four bulls.

The marshal was therefore executed, and the King gave his daughter to Baldwyn, and named him his viceroy over the whole kingdom. The wedding was celebrated with great joy, and the young King caused his father and his foster-father to be brought, and loaded them with treasures.

Neither did he forget the inn-keeper, but sent for him and said, "Behold, sir host, I have married the King's daughter, and your house and yard are mine."

The host said, "Yes, according to justice it is so." But the young King said, "It shall be done according to mercy," and told him that he should keep his house and yard, and gave him the thousand pieces of gold as well.

The Forest Enchantments[75]

And now the young twin and his bride were thoroughly happy, and lived in gladness together. He often went out hunting because it was a delight to him, and the faithful animals had to accompany him.

In the neighborhood, however, there was a forest of which it was reported that it was haunted, and that whosoever did but enter it did not easily get out again. Baldwyn however had a great inclination to hunt in it, and let the old King have no peace until he allowed him to do so.

So he rode forth with a great following, and when he came to the forest, he saw a snow-white hart grazing and said to his people, "Wait here until I return, I want to chase that beautiful creature," and he rode into the forest after it, followed only by his animals.

The attendants halted and waited until evening, but he did not return, so they rode home, and told the young bride that her husband had followed a white hart into the enchanted forest, and had not come back again.

Then Tugenda was in the greatest concern about him.

Baldwyn however had still continued to ride on and on after the beautiful wild animal, and had never been able to overtake it; when he thought he was near enough to aim, he instantly saw it bound away into the far distance, and at length it vanished altogether.

And now he perceived that he had penetrated deep into the forest, and blew his horn. But he received no answer, for his attendants could not hear it.

And as night, too, was falling, he saw that he could not get home that day, so he dismounted from his horse, lighted himself a fire near a tree, and resolved to spend the night by it.

While he was sitting by the fire, and his animals also were lying down beside him, it seemed to him that he heard a human voice. He looked round, but could perceive nothing.

Soon afterwards, he again heard a groan as if from above, and then he looked up, and saw an old woman sitting in the tree, who wailed unceasingly, "Oh, oh, oh, how cold I am!"

Said he, "Come down, and warm yourself if you are cold."

But she said, "No, your animals will bite me."

He answered, "They will do you no harm, old mother, do come down."

She, however, was a witch, and said, "I will throw down a wand from the tree, and if you strike them on the back with it, they will do me no harm."

Then she threw him a small wand, and he struck them with it, and instantly they lay still and were turned into stone.

And when the witch was safe from the animals, she leapt down and touched him also with her wand, and changed him to stone also.

Thereupon she laughed, and dragged him and the animals into a great underground vault, where many more such stones already lay.

As, however, the husband did not come back at all, the bride's anguish and care grew constantly greater.

Ye Shrewed Awakening

The Princess[76]

It came to pass that old King Ultman's remaining daughter, Galiana, still beautiful beyond all measure, but at the same time so proud and arrogant that no suitor was good enough for her. She rejected one after the other, ridiculing them as well.

In frustration, the old king sponsored a great feast and invited from far and near all suitable men wanting for marriage. At introduction time, they were all placed in a row according to their rank and standing. First came the Kings, then the grand dukes, then the princes, the earls, the barons, and the aristocracy.

Then the king's daughter was led through the ranks, but she objected to something about each one.

One was too fat and feral: "The wild wine barrel," she said.

Another was too tall: "Thin and tall, no good at all."

The third was too short: "Short and thick is never quick."

The fourth was too pale: "As death is stale."

The fifth too red: "A prize rooster to dread."

The sixth was not straight enough: "Green wood, dried behind the stove."

The seventh was too old: "Smelled of mold".

And thus she had some objection to each one. But she ridiculed especially one good king who stood at the very top of the row, and whose chin had hair grown a little crooked.

"Look!" she cried out, laughing, "He has a beard like a thrush's beak."

And from that time he was called, "*King Thrushbeard*".

A Suitor[77]

Now the old king, seeing that his daughter did nothing but ridicule the people, making fun of all the suitors who were gathered there, became very angry. And in that moment, he swore that she should have for her husband the very first beggar to come to his door.

A few days later a minstrel came a singing beneath the king's window, trying to earn a small handout.

When King Ultman heard him he said, "Let him come up at once."

So the minstrel, in his dirty, ragged clothes, came in and sang before the king and his daughter, and when he was finished he asked for a small gift.

The king said, "I liked your song so much that I will give you my daughter for a wife."

Galiana took fright, but the king said, "I have taken an oath to give you to the very first beggar, and I will keep it."

The Honeymoon[78]

Her protests did not help in the least. The priest was called in, and she had to marry the lowly minstrel at once.

Afterward the king said, "It is not proper for you, a beggar's wife, to stay in my palace any longer. All you can do now is to go away with your husband."

The beggar led her out by the hand, and she had to leave with him, walking on foot.

They came to a large forest, and she asked, "Who owns this beautiful forest?"

"It belongs to King Thrushbeard. If you had taken him, it would be yours."

"Oh, I am a miserable thing;" she cried out,
"If only I'd taken the Thrushbeard King."

Afterwards they crossed a lush meadow, and she asked again, "Who owns this beautiful green meadow?"

"It belongs to King Thrushbeard. If you had taken him, it would be yours."

"Oh, I am a miserable thing;" she cried out a
second time, "If only I'd taken the
Thrushbeard King."

Then they walked through a large town, and she asked again, "Who owns this beautiful large town?"

"It belongs to King Thrushbeard. If you had taken him, it would be yours."

"Oh, I am a miserable thing;" she cried out a third time, "If only I'd taken the Thrushbeard King."

"I do not like you to always be wishing for another husband," said the minstrel. "Am I not good enough for you?"

A Return Home[79]

At last they came to a very little hut, and Galiana said, "Oh goodness. What a small house. Who owns this miserable tiny hut?"

The minstrel answered, "This is my house and yours, where we shall live together."

She was not at all pleased and had to stoop in order to get through the low door.

"Where are the servants?" said Galiana.

"What servants?" answered the beggar.

"Why those who would do my bidding!" she exclaimed.

"You must do for yourself what you want to have done. Now make a fire at once, put some water on to boil, so you can cook me something to eat. I am very tired" he said.

But Galiana knew nothing about lighting fires or cooking, and the minstrel in the end had to lend a hand himself to get anything done at all.

When they had finished their scanty meal they went to bed. But he made her get up very early the next morning in order to do the housework.

Trial & Error[80]

For a few days they lived in this way, and as well as they could, but they finally came to the end of their provisions and were then in need.

The man said, "Wife, we cannot go on any longer eating and drinking here and earning nothing. You must weave baskets to market for sale." He went out, cut some willows, and brought them home.

Then she began to weave baskets, but the hard willows cut into her delicate hands.

"I see that this will not do," said the man. "You had better spin. Perhaps you can do that better."

Galiana sat down and tried to spin, but the hard thread soon cut into her soft fingers until they bled.

"See," said the man. "You are not good for any sort of work. I made a bad bargain with you. Now I will try to start a business with pots and earthenware. You must sit in the marketplace and sell them."

"Oh!" Galiana thought. "If people from my father's realm come to the market and see me sitting there selling things, how they will ridicule me!"

But her protests did not help her. She had to do what her husband demanded, for she did not want to die of hunger.

The Calamity[81]

At first it went well. People bought the woman's wares because she was beautiful, and they paid Galiana whatever she asked. Many even gave her the money and let her keep the pots.

So they lived on what she earned as long as it lasted.

Then the husband bought a lot of new pottery. She sat down with this at the corner of the marketplace and set it around her for sale.

But suddenly there came a drunken hussar galloping along, and he rode right into the pots, breaking them into a thousand pieces.

She began to cry, and was so afraid that she did not know what to do.

"Oh! What will happen to me?" she cried. "What will my husband say about this?"

She ran home and told him of the misfortune.

"Who would sit at the corner of the marketplace with earthenware?" said the man.

"Now stop crying. I see very well that you are not fit for any ordinary work. Now I was at our king's palace and asked if they couldn't use a kitchen maid. They promised me to take you. In return you will get free food."

The king's daughter now became a kitchen maid, and had to be available to the cook, and to do the dirtiest work.

In each of Galiana's pockets she fastened a little jar, in which she took home her share of the leftovers.

And this is what they lived on.

A Comeuppance[82]

Back in the tyrant's realm, in his flight, the mercenary had forgotten the most valuable things he had – the blue light, flute and the gold. Worse still, Helmer had only one ducat in his pocket.

And now loaded with chains, he was standing at the window of his dungeon, when he chanced to see one of his comrades passing by. The mercenary tapped at the pane of glass, and when this man came up, said to him: "Be so kind as to fetch me the small bundle I have left lying in the inn, and I will give you a ducat for doing it."

The journeyman replied, "Keep your money good friend for I have no need of it and am in good cheer. Trust that I shall have your bundle to you in no time."

Brother Lustig took to his errand and waiting till he was out of sight, he wished the bundle to his knapsack and soon brought it to the mercenary without haste.

As soon as the mercenary was alone again, he played his flute and summoned the gnome. "Have no fear," said the latter to his master.

"Go wheresoever they take you, and let them do what they will, only take the blue light with you."

Next day the mercenary was tried, and though he had done nothing unjust, the judge condemned him to death.

When he was led forth to die, he begged a last favor of the tyrant.

"What is it?" asked the tyrant.

"That I may play one more tune on my flute."

"You may play three," answered the tyrant, "but do not imagine that I will spare your life."

Then the mercenary pulled out his flute and played it at the blue light, and as soon as a few notes had been played, the manikin was there with a small cudgel in his hand, and said: "What does my lord command?"

"Strike down to earth that false judge there, and his constable, and spare not the tyrant who has treated me so ill."

Then the gnome fell on them like lightning, darting this way and that way, and whosoever was so much as touched by his cudgel fell to earth, and did not venture to stir again.

The tyrant was terrified; he threw himself on Helmer's mercy, and merely to be allowed to live at all, gave him his realm for his own, and his daughter to wife.

From The East[83]

And it so happened that at this very time the other twin who had turned to the east when they separated, came into King Wilford's realm. Odwin had sought a situation, and had found none, and had then travelled about here and there, and had made his animals dance.

Then it came into his mind that he would just go and look at the knife that they had thrust in the trunk of a tree at their parting, that he might learn how his twin brother was.

When he got there his brother's side of the knife was half rusted, and half bright.

Then he was alarmed and thought, "A great misfortune must have befallen my brother, but perhaps I can still save him, for half the knife is still bright."

He and his animals travelled with great haste towards the west, and when he entered the gate of the town, the guard came to meet him, and asked if he was to announce him to his consort the young bride, who had for a couple of days been in the greatest sorrow about his staying away, and was afraid he had been killed in the enchanted forest.

The sentries, indeed, thought no otherwise than that he was the young husband himself, for he looked so like him, and had wild animals running behind him.

Then he saw that they were speaking of his brother, and thought, "It will be better if I pass myself off for him, and then I can rescue him more easily."

So Odwin allowed himself to be escorted into the castle by the guard, and was received with the greatest joy.

The young bride indeed thought too that he was her young king and husband, and asked him why he had stayed away so long.

Odwin answered, "I had lost myself in a forest, and could not find my way out again any sooner."

At night he was taken to the royal bed, but he laid a two-edged sword between[pp] him and the young bride; Tugenda did not know what it meant, and did not dare to ask.

A Forest Rescue[84]

The twin's brother remained in the palace a couple of days, and in the meantime inquired into everything which related to the enchanted forest, and at last Odwin said, "I must hunt there once more."

The old King and the young bride wanted to persuade him not to do it, but he stood out against them, and went forth with a larger following.

[pp] It is a custom within some cultures to convey to one's bed partner one's unavailability by placing an obstruction between the partner and oneself while in bed.

When Odwin had got into the forest, it fared with him as with his brother; he saw a snow-white hart and said to his people, "Stay here, and wait until I return, I want to chase the lovely wild beast," and then he rode into the forest and his animals ran after him.

But he could not overtake the hart, and got so deep into the forest that he was forced to pass the night there.

And when he had lighted a fire, he heard someone wailing above him, "Oh, oh, oh, how cold I am!"

Then he looked up, and the self-same witch was sitting in the tree. Said he, "If you are cold, come down, little old mother, and warm thyself."

She answered, "No, your animals will bite me."

But he said, "They will not hurt you."

Then she cried, "I will throw down a wand to you, and if you smite them with it they will do me no harm."

When the huntsman heard that, he had no confidence in the old woman, and said, "I will not strike my animals. Come down, or I will fetch you."

Then she cried, "What do you want? You shall not touch me."

But suspecting her a witch now he replied, "If you do not come, I will shoot you."

Said she, "Shoot away, I do not fear your bullets!"

Knowing no good would come from her, he aimed, and fired at her, but the witch was proof against all leaden bullets, and laughed, and yelled and cried, "You shall not hit me."

Odwin knew what to do. He tore three silver buttons off his coat, and loaded his gun with them, for against them her arts were useless, and when he fired she fell down at once with a scream.

Then he set his foot upon her and said, "Old witch, if you do not instantly confess where my brother is, I will seize you with both my hands and throw you into the fire."

She was in a great fright, begged for mercy and said, "He and his animals lie turned to stone in an underground vault."

Then he compelled her to go thither with him, threatened her, and said, "Old sea-cat, now shall you make my brother and all the human beings lying here, alive again, or you shall go into the fire!"

She took a wand and touched the stones, and then his brother with his animals came to life again, and many others, merchants, artisans, and shepherds, arose, thanked him for their deliverance, and went to their homes.

But when the twin brothers saw each other again, they hugged and kissed each other and rejoiced with all their hearts.

Then they seized the witch, bound her and laid her on the fire, and when she was burnt to ash and scattered by the four winds, the forest opened of its own accord, and was light and clear, and the King's palace could be seen at about the distance of a three hours walk.

The Celebration[85]

In other parts, it happened soon after that Galiana took to working in the castle that the wedding of the monarch's eldest son was to be celebrated, so the poor woman went up and stood near the door of the hall to look on.

When all the lights were lit, and people, each more beautiful than the other, entered, and all was full of pomp and splendor, she thought about her plight with a sad heart, and cursed the pride and haughtiness which had humbled her and brought her to such great poverty.

The smell of the delicious dishes which were being taken in and out reached her, and now and then the servants threw her a few scraps, which she put in her jar to take home.

Then suddenly the monarch's son entered, clothed in velvet and silk, with gold chains around his neck.

When he saw the beautiful woman standing by the door he took her by the hand and wanted danced with her. But she refused and took fright, for she saw that he was King Thrushbeard, the suitor whom she had rejected with scorn.

Galiana's struggles did not help her. He pulled her into the hall. But the string that tied up her pockets broke, and the pots fell to the floor. The soup ran out, and the scraps flew everywhere.

When the people saw this, everyone laughed and ridiculed her. She was so ashamed that she would rather have been a thousand fathoms beneath the ground.

She jumped out the door and wanted to run away, but a man overtook her on the stairs and brought her back. And when she looked at him, it was King Thrushbeard again.

He said to her kindly, "Don't be afraid. I and the minstrel who has been living with you in that miserable hut are one and the same. For the love of you I disguised myself. And I was also the hussar who broke your pottery to pieces. All this was done to humble your proud spirit and to punish you for the arrogance with which you ridiculed me."

Then Galiana cried bitterly and said, "I was terribly wrong, and am not worthy to be your wife."

But he said, "Be comforted. The evil days are past. Now we will celebrate our wedding."

Then the maids-in-waiting came and dressed her in the most splendid clothing, and her father and his whole court came and wished her happiness in her marriage with King Thrushbeard, and their true happiness began only now.

Regrets[86]

Back in the forest, after destroying the witch, the two twin brothers went home together, and on the way told each other their histories. And when the youngest said that he was Viceroy of the whole country in the King's stead, the other observed, "That I remarked very well, for when I came to the town, and was taken for you, all royal honors were paid me; your young bride looked on me as her husband, and I had to eat at her side, and sleep in your bed."

When the other heard that, he became so jealous and angry that he drew his sword, and struck off his brother's head.

But when he saw him lying there dead, and saw his red blood flowing, he repented most violently: "My

brother delivered me," cried he, "and I have killed him for it," and he bewailed him aloud.

Then his hare came and offered to go and bring some of the root of life, and bounded away and brought it while yet there was time, and the dead man was brought to life again, and knew nothing about the wound.

Homeward Bound[87]

After this they journeyed onwards, and Baldwyn said, "You look like me, have royal apparel on as I have, and the animals follow you as they do me; we will go in by opposite gates, and arrive at the same time from the two sides in the aged King's presence."

So they separated, and at the same time came the watchmen from the one door and from the other, and announced that the young King and the animals had returned from the chase.

The old King said, "It is not possible, the gates lie quite a mile apart."

In the meantime, however, the two brothers entered the courtyard of the palace from opposite sides, and both mounted the steps.

Then the old King said to the daughter, "Say which is thy husband. Each of them looks exactly like the other, I cannot tell."

Then Tugenda was in great distress, and could not tell; but at last she remembered the necklace which she had given to the animals, and she sought for and found her little golden clasp on the lion, and she cried in her delight, "He who is followed by this lion is my true husband."

Then Baldwyn laughed and said, "Yes, I am the right one," and they sat down together to table, and ate and drank, and were merry.

At night when the young king went to bed, his wife said, "Why have you for these last nights always laid a two-edged sword in our bed? I thought you had a wish to kill me."

Then he knew how true his brother had been.

The Gates of Heaven[88]

It was not till years later that an old Brother Lustig came upon heaven's gate, where he knocked with weary zeal. The pious master, who had entered through heaven's gate long before, was sitting hard by as its door-keeper.

The old journeyman recognized him at once, and thought, "Here at last I find an old friend, I shall get on better."

But Achim said, "I really believe that you want to enter this gate into Heaven."

"Then let me in, my good brother; I must get in somewhere; if they would have taken me into hell, I should not have come here."

"No, my dear ruffian" said the pious master, "You shall not enter here."

"Then if you will not let me in, take your knapsack back, for I will have nothing at all from you."

"I accept. Now give it me," said Achim.

Then the old journeyman gave him the knapsack through the bars of heaven's gate, and the pious master took it and hung it beside his seat.

Then, thinking he had outsmarted the gatekeeper, Brother Lustig said, "Aha! Now I wish myself inside my knapsack."

But the old journeyman was so entrenched on his path that instead of finding himself inside the gates of heaven, the knapsack leaped from its hook and found itself hoodwinking the old journeyman's head.

"Well!", Brother Lustig thought, removing his knapsack from his startled face, "That was most unexpected!"

But he continued with excitement saying loudly to himself, "Now *there's* a tale I wish were in my knapsack."

And no sooner had his words spilled from his mouth when he heard a rustling from within his knapsack.

A Tale to Be Told[89]

Curious as to what had come to his knapsack by his words, Brother Lustig opened it only to see to his surprise parchments lying within. The old relic eagerly reached in, pulled them out to the light of day and began reading...

There was once upon a time a young lad who loved hearing stories...

Appendices

A. Journeyman

(noun)

a) a trained worker employed by someone else.
b) a person hired to do work for another, usually for a day at a time.
c) a skilled artisan who works on hire for master artisans rather than for himself.
d) a person who has served an apprenticeship at a trade or handicraft and is certified to work at it assisting or under another person.
e) an individual who has completed an apprenticeship and is fully educated in a trade or craft, but is not yet a master.
f) a craftsman, artisan, etc, who is qualified to work at his trade in the employment of another.
g) any experienced, competent but routine worker or performer.
h) a worker, performer, or sports player who is reliable, experienced and good but not outstanding or excellent.
i) a competent but not excellent workman.
j) [formerly] a worker hired on a daily wage. Day Worker
k) A mature traveler, explorer, and adventurer

Synonyms: day worker, jack, knave, fellow craft, tradesman, worker, artisan, craftsman, skilled worker, artisan, machinist, maker, manufacturer, mechanic, smith, technician, wright

Origin: 1425–75; late Middle English: from journey (in the obsolete sense 'day's work') + man; so named because the journeyman was no longer bound by indentures but was paid by the day. Equivalent to *journee* (a day's work) + man

B. Journey Flow Chart

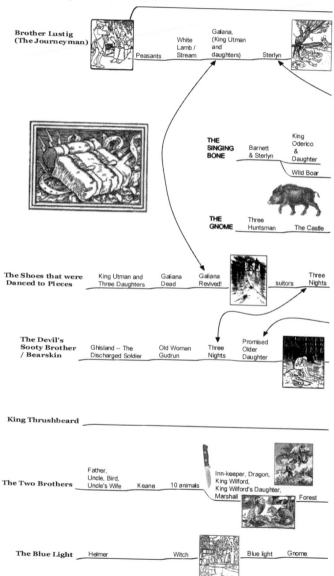

Brother Lustig (The Journeyman) — Peasants — White Lamb / Stream — Galana, (King Utman and daughters) — Sterlyn

THE SINGING BONE — Barnett & Sterlyn — King Oderico & Daughter — Wild Boar

THE GNOME — Three Huntsman — The Castle

The Shoes that were Danced to Pieces — King Utman and Three Daughters — Galiana Dead — Galiana Revived! — suitors — Three Nights

The Devil's Sooty Brother / Bearskin — Ghisland -- The Discharged Soldier — Old Woman Gudrun — Three Nights — Promised Older Daughter

King Thrushbeard _____

The Two Brothers — Father, Uncle, Bird, Uncle's Wife — Keane — 10 animals — Inn-keeper, Dragon, King Wilford, King Wilford's Daughter, Marshall — Forest

The Blue Light — Helmer — Witch — Blue light — Gnome

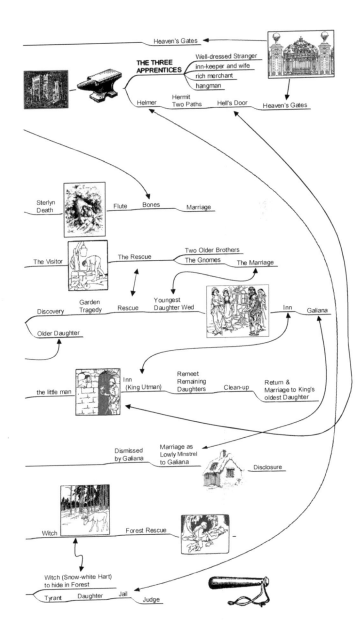

Heaven's Gates

THE THREE APPRENTICES

Well-dressed Stranger
inn-keeper and wife
rich merchant
hangman

Helmer   Hermit   Hell's Door   Heaven's Gates
          Two Paths

Sterlyn   Flute   Bones   Marriage
Death

The Visitor   The Rescue   Two Older Brothers
                             The Gnomes   The Marriage

Discovery   Garden   Rescue   Youngest   Inn   Galiana
             Tragedy   Daughter Wed

Older Daughter

the little man   Inn   Remeet   Clean-up   Return &
                 (King Utman) Remaining   Marriage to King's
                             Daughters   oldest Daughter

                 Dismissed   Marriage as
                 by Galiana   Lowly Minstrel
                              to Galiana   Disclosure

Witch   Forest Rescue

Witch (Snow-white Hart)
to hide in Forest
Tyrant   Daughter   Jail   Judge

C. Bibliography and Resources

1) **King, Warrior, Magician, Lover: Rediscovering the Archetypes of the Mature Masculine** – Robert L. Moore, Doug Gillette; Harper San Francisco, 1991, 160 pages
2) **A Gathering of Men** – Robert Bly and Bill Moyers PBS Production, 1990
3) **Brother Lustig** – Grimm, Jacob and Wilhelm. *Household Tales*. Margaret Hunt, translator. London: George Bell, 1884, 1892. 2 volumes.
4) **The Two Brothers** – ibid
5) **The Singing Bone** – ibid
6) **The Blue Light** – ibid[qq]
7) **The Three Apprentices** – ibid
8) **The Shoes That Were Danced to Pieces** – ibid
9) **The Gnome** – ibid
10) **Bearskin** – ibid
11) **The Devil's Sooty Brother** – ibid
12) **King Thrushbeard** – ibid

[qq] NOTES: The Blue Light – From the province of Mecklenburg. The pipe which the soldier smokes [in other variations of this story], must have had its origin in the flute, which the elves are elsewhere accustomed to obey... . The blue light is a will-o'-the-wisp, Danish vättelys (spirit-light), and Lygtemand, the Lord of the little dwarf. Schärtlin's exclamation was "Blue fire!" which words too are several times to be found in *Hans Sacks*. ... In Danish, see the *Tinder-box*, in Andersen, vol. i. In Hungarian, *The Tobacco-Pipe*...

D. About the Author

Professionally, John S. Nagy is a multi degree professional business and life coach, technical advisor, trainer, lecturer, speaker and writer who provides coaching, management and technical support to business professionals worldwide. He has been in the coaching field since 1989, running his own coaching practice since that time.

His coaching oriented corporation (Coaching for Success, Inc.) operates on the principles he asks his own clients to practice. Coach Nagy started his organization with a rich background of experience in the business development, project management and consulting fields. He specializes in management systems evaluation and process development. John has a strong tendency of keeping people in action toward worthwhile goals that are clearly identified and to which they are committed to bring about more effectively.

Coach Nagy is also a State Certified County Mediator in Florida. He mediates court ordered cases part time in the 13th Judicial Circuit of Hillsborough County.

John has been a published author since the early 1990's, writing and publishing many articles, books and booklets on personal and professional development. His materials are used to instruct individuals in professional and personal development. This includes *Symbol Recognition, Understanding and Application* toward living better, more productive and enjoyable lives.

You can find out more about Coach Nagy, his services, his books, his videos and his workshops through his website page found at:

http://www.coach.net

E. Lessons, Points & Fodder to Ponder

The tale that is told is filled with many lessons ready for the taking. You could read this story only for pure pleasure and obtain tremendous value from this action alone. Should you want more though, and wish to explore the rich symbolism the tale has to offer as a way of stimulating personal transformation, below are many opportunities for you to seek, learn and grow for the better. They are only presented here as tinder though, so if you wish to have a much bigger fire, add to these offerings as your heart desires and your spirit demands.

It is recommended you explore this section only after you read the tale through completely.

---

1 As written within the book, *King Warrior Magician Lover*, they represent the four Mature Masculine Archetypes. What can you share about these archetypes and their immature counterparts?

2 Often times we are discharged or dismissed from our duties and life's work, even after doing everything right. What naturally occurs within one's own heart and mind at these events and during these times of transition?

3 Although we are at times limited in what we have, there are those who have far less. How do you respond to those who ask you to share your hard earned resources? What must be present

for you to share?

4 There are times when you are without resources. How do you respond to requests when you have nothing to offer? When offered opportunities to travel together for mutual support, how do you proceed?

5 Great stresses bring about desperate behaviors. How do you react to the cries of others? When confronted with antagonistic ends, how do you negotiate respectfully with others to have your needs met in honorable ways?

6 The value of a man's word is directly proportional to how it shall be kept once given and how accurate it is once manifested. How valuable is your word?

   Temperance in one's behavior is a virtue. How do you keep yourself within due bounds, especially when you are working with others? How do your needs override your agreements?

7 Denying reality can damage relationships. What is your typical behavior when confronted with what you do not want to hear?

8 Conditions arise when you must choose between your preferred self-image and how the world actually sees you. Would you risk death denying how you are and what you have done?

9 We shall often be present to the great works of others. How do you make effort to receive rewards for their works?

10 Reality has a way of presenting us options where we willingly change our words to match it, even when what we have professed previously is now in question. How have you

willingly changed your words to suit situations so you may benefit at the cost of your word?

11 Life provides us many valuable opportunities where we may benefit ourselves or unknowingly benefit others to our detriment. What valuable opportunities have you passed up not initially recognizing the true value that was given to you?

12 Sometimes our best delegated plans do not come out as imagined. Have you ever delegated something to another and didn't get what you wanted because the person doing the work did not know your end in mind?

Life has a way of blessing us in unexpected ways. What blessings can you recall that came to you just because you were at the right place at the right time?

There are people who are not after our best interests. What situations can you recall where you were persuaded into giving something up that you would have not done so had you known better?

13 There exist good people in the world who want nothing but the best for others. How many people can you recall that took you under their tutelage because you were in need and they could help you?

14 Taking a different path often affords different opportunities. What opportunities have you been blessed with by simply taking a different path or going in a different direction?

15 Being too trusting of our familiars sometimes sets us up for very damaging consequences. In

whom have you placed your trust that ultimately proved to be costly to you?

Situations sometimes unfold where we can take advantage of another's valiant efforts. When have you taken advantage of another's hard work and done so to their detriment?

16 The world has a way of revealing the truth. What truths have you made effort to cover up that were eventually brought to the light of day? How did you deal with the revelations once known by all?

17 Opportunities in life best serve the prepared. What opportunities have you attempted to take advantage of where you were sadly ill-prepared?

18 Situations occur when rescuers appear unexpectedly. What situations have you gotten yourself into where it is clear to you that you are better off this day because someone intervened for your benefit?

19 There are some people who shall never fully comprehend how they lack integrity but are generally benign in their activities. How to you treat these people, especially when they have broken their promises to you?

20 Eventually, what you prepare for shall be put to test. What are you preparing for and when do you believe that you shall be ready?

21 There comes a point in everyone's life when they realize they have learned all that they can where they are and need to leave the security of their teachers to experience further growth. What points in your life have you realized this

and have taken action toward this end?

22 Having people in our lives who want nothing but our best for us and take action to make sure this becomes possible is a blessing for anyone to have. What people do you know who want nothing but your best for you and take action to assure this occurs for you?

23 There occurs in everyone's life a parting of ways due to an inability to serve further for one reason or another. What have you done in these instances and how have things worked out?

24 Descending into the unknown for mercenary reasons is sometimes met with unexpected results upon returning. When have you been met with individuals so greedy for what you have that your own welfare was never their concern?

25 There are countless opportunities to take advantage of others good resources without their knowledge. How do you temper what is offered to you with ethical behavior and moral guidance?

26 Accepting the kindness of strangers is not without its risks. How willing are you to risk accepting gifts not knowing if such gifts come with possible harm?

27 Delayed gratification for better returns is a discipline that not many develop. How willing are you to delay immediate gratification not knowing if such a delay will bring about your needs being met in abundance?

28 We are sometimes called to separate from our family and friends. How do you usually

respond?

29 Adventures sometimes require us to enter into situations where we face potential danger and hardship. When told that you are about to engage in situations where few have succeeded, how do you prepare yourself?

30 There are shadows in everyone's lives. When faced with yours, what actions do you take to deal with them effectively?

31 It's not enough to capture your shadows. How do you divest yourself of them once you capture them?

32 There are many paths in life and each one leads us somewhere. What path are you currently on and is it taking you where you want to go?

33 Opportunities knock in many forms especially when we least expect them and at times when we are most desperate. How willing are you to parrot things that you know nothing of simply for the promise of potential reward?

34 Life is filled with situations that seem insane. How do you typically make sense of things that don't come across well-founded?

35 Challenging work is always available to those who seek it. When a challenge presents itself to you, do you back away from it or do you approach it head on?

36 Life's dragons come in all shapes and sizes. How do you go about effectively dealing with the dragons in your life?

37 Each of us has many aspects of our nature. What aspects of your nature can you readily identify?

Rest is an important aspect of recuperation. When you need to recuperate, whom do you put in charge to safeguard all that you have worked hard to achieve?

38 Situations sometimes cut us off from our thinking, especially when we believe the dangers we just faced are danger's end. What dangerous situations do you create for yourself when you seek recuperation and shut off your thinking?

39 Aspects of our nature awaken at different times and in turn each has different ways of assisting us toward awakening and healing. What do you believe are your natural aspects, how do they help you awaken and how do they help you heal?

40 Change is constant and we can easily have our heads turned around by unanticipated events. What view do you have when you're head is turned around and what do you know you must do to get your head back on straight?

41 Parroting response to life's demands often leads us into situations that bind us beyond our usual tolerations. How does parroting serve good purpose and when does it cause very binding problems.

42 Keeping our word true is an important part of our integrity. How does keeping our word true, despite insurmountable reasons to break it, serve your good?

43 Revenge is ultimately damaging to all it touches. How willing are you to allow innocent people to be used and possibly abused and

harmed by your vengeful efforts?

44 Mysteries surround us from every side. What are you willing to give of yourself to have answers to those situations that puzzle you most?

45 There are times when we are left with the impression that we are not needed or wanted, and sometimes by those we would hope would never give that impression. When have you experienced this and how did you deal effectively with these situations?

46 Assistance comes in unexpected ways and that assistance sometimes requires a promise in return. What future promises have you made in return for present assistance?

47 Planning is a very good way of living through situations where you think you have no control. How do you go about planning for changes?

48 Adventure and mystery go hand in hand when life is lived to its fullest. How willing are you to engage in life's adventures when you know that its mysteries might be revealed to you?

49 Testimonials are not always easy things in which to participate. When presented opportunities to testify as to what you have witnessed, do you stick to the facts or do you have a point to prove that goes beyond presenting them?

50 Arrogance is acting as if the rules do not apply to you. How has arrogance played out in your life and what were the consequences for disregarding or making effort to usurp the rules?

51 Quests may present many resources that support them. How do you take advantage of the resources that present themselves once you commit to any important undertaking?

52 Not all victims are so by outside influences; some are this way by their own creation. How have you ever tried to assist someone only to find that they were setting you up to be a victim yourself?

53 Life is filled with many disappointments. How have you trained yourself to deal with these situations effectively?

54 Life requires us to go deep into things and for all the right reasons. In what situations have you invested yourself deeply and for all the right reasons?

55 Going deep into things gets us in touch with treasures not available on the surface. What treasures have you obtained by purposely going below the surface?

56 Taking time to stoke our personal fires with the expressed intent to boil things down to their essence is a time honored tradition for many who seek beneficial transformation. What time do you invest boiling down past experiences in your life to obtain a clearer understanding of the lessons that were offered and insights into changes that need to occur?

57 It is a practice in some cultures to take one year to grieve a loss. How much time do you take to properly come to acceptance?

58 Life demands we subdue our natural aspects. Can you subdue yours toward beneficial ends?

59 Symbols are often used as a way of letting others know specific information and associations. What symbols can you readily identify that tell you specific information and associations that enable you to make better choices?

Mastery takes many forms and can be directed toward many ends. What have you mastered?

60 We each have natural aspects that enable us to achieve things that others could not begin to imagine. What aspects of your nature enable you to obtain your goals with little to no efforts?

61 Some of our more powerful natures come to our service when they are properly directed. What successes have you had with directing them?

62 The sweeter side of life is often only experienced by expressing our powerful natures. What have you had to express to experience life's sweetness?

63 The spiritual side of life is often experienced through great courage. How courageous have you been in life and what spiritual aspects have you experienced as a result?

64 Confidence reflects certainty over specific conditions. What must you have before you and within you to remain confident in your everyday dealings?

65 Investment sometimes requires we risk being rejected by that which we seek. What desires have you sought that closed doors initially?

66 Our personal shadows block access into even the darkest recesses of our soul. What personal

shadows prevent you from venturing forth into your darkest regions?

67 Even when we believe we have served our proper time to accomplish something of significance, there still remain specific boundaries we must cross to arrive at where we need to be. What situations have you been involved in that left you wanting even though you believed you fulfilled what was required to obtain something of great importance?

Our own misconceptions and preconceived notions can keep us prisoner long after we no longer are held to our agreements. What holds you back from living the life you believe you deserve?

68 We are provided endless opportunities to honor our promises and obligations toward ourselves and others. How many situations have you noticed this and took actions in the direction you knew would honor your word to yourself and others?

69 Even in our most awful looking states there are people who see past our superficial aspects and into the core of our being. How often are you surprised by how people either respond to your inner appearance or react to your outer appearance?

70 It's rare that others shall demand from you with such clarity and depth of purpose what you should demand from yourself. What turning points were presented in your life where your insights and personal demands transformed your very being in an instance?

71 There are times when we must return to places we have been before due to promises we have made to ourselves and others. What returning opportunities have you created for yourself to revisit past situations and fulfill long standing obligations?

72 Life has a way of opening doors thought long closed. What doors have closed for you in your past and how have you prepared yourself for their eventual re-openings?

73 Moments present themselves that provide opportunity to reveal truths. How do you go about assuring that your Light shines without flicker?

74 If inner peace is to come forth, debts are to be repaid in life or forgiven. How do you go about making or accepting payment for those debts owed?

75 Life's enchantments compel us toward unexpected ends. What enchantments have caused you to become bound up as a result of poor choices?

76 There exist souls who judge based upon very superficial criteria. Whom have you had judge you superficially in your life and how did you deal with their judgments?

77 We may wear many masks in our dealings with others. With what masks have you adorned yourself pursuing your desires and taking advantage of situations that require it?

78 We are sometimes confronted with what we have given up or lost as a consequence of foolish pride. What situations have you been

confronted with that reflected major loss due to
your arrogance?

79 Maturity requires taking responsibility for
burdening yourself with life supporting tasks.
What situations have you had to take upon
yourself to engage in a mature life?

80 Life requires that we be open to learning new
skills and such activities often require building
up a tolerance for what we must engage. In
what new activities have you made effort to
engage that caused you some initial
discomfort?

81 Not all people want us to succeed in the
directions we find ourselves going. In what
specific situations have you felt sabotaged by
others in your attempts to succeed?

82 Our greatest skills and blessings need not be
shared overtly with everyone. Have you ever
disclosed a blessing only to have it taken from
you?

   Opportunities for revenge present themselves
to us endlessly, especially when one holds a
vengeful spirit. When provided chances to exact
revenge, how does your heart direct your
actions?

83 We come to situations where people might
mistake us for whom they truly believe is before
them. Do you take advantage of such situations
to the detriment of those involved or do you
fully respect whom you represent and take no
action that is not honorable to those involved?

84 Things tend to replay in our lives. From what
previously presented lessons have you learned

so well that when they present themselves once again you make much better choices?

85 We may go to some extremes making efforts to survive in life; doing things that we would not imagine doing. What situations have you found yourself in where you felt overwhelmingly embarrassed by your activities?

86 Impulse control is one of the attributes of a mature spirit. What impulses have you acted upon only to find you have destroyed what you love most by doing so?

87 We often do not discover until much later how loyalty plays out in our lives. What situations have you experienced where you discovered the depth of your friend's loyalties long after actions occurred?

88 We sometimes believe we can prevent ourselves from suffering the consequences of well-entrenched behaviors. What consequences have you made effort to avoid knowing full well that they were a direct result of your unchecked behavior?

89 Surprises come to us in many different ways. What are those surprises that you have experienced which have left you with a warm glow afterward?

- Find Your Way -

Made in the USA
Charleston, SC
15 December 2016